Mr. Pinkerton

Twenty four short stories

By

Gillian Jackson

Published in 2014 by FeedARead.com Publishing

Copyright © The author as named on the book cover.

The author or authors assert their moral right under the Copyright, Designs and Patents Act, 1988, to be identified as the author or authors of this work.

All Rights reserved. No part of this publication may be reproduced, copied, stored in a retrieval system, or transmitted, in any form or by any means, without the prior written consent of the copyright holder, nor be otherwise circulated in any form of binding or cover other than that in which it is published and without a similar condition being imposed on the subsequent purchaser.

A CIP catalogue record for this title is available from the British Library.

Contents

Mr Pinkerton
Underground
Picture Perfect
Say it with Flowers
Old Friends
The Lift
True Identity
I Wish...
One Step at a Time
With Love
Waiting
The Bridge
A Good Day's Work
Coming of Age
Always the Bridesmaid
Poor Malcolm
Chain Reaction
London Lifestyles
The Postman's Daughter
The Interview
It's All in the Planning
The Desk
Imagination
Happy New Year

Mr. Pinkerton

Decorum abandoned, the two sixty-something women were giggling like school girls.

Irene's hand dithered over the plate of biscuits in front of her, finally deciding on a half coated chocolate digestive.
"It's apathy!" Maureen declared, helping herself to two biscuits.
"Everyone wants the benefits of living in a nice place like this, but no one is prepared to accept any of the responsibilities." She again droned on about her favourite subject while Irene sipped the tea, feigning interest in what she had heard at least a dozen times before.
"I'm quite happy to continue as secretary of the residents' committee for another year, but we really must have a new chairman. I can't keep on doing both jobs."
Irene nodded in agreement, hoping Maureen wasn't expecting her to volunteer for the role, heaven forbid. She hated anything to do with committees and found it difficult enough to choose what to have for her next meal.
"Why, I think I could even nominate Mr. Pinkerton here and no one would be any the wiser!" Maureen broke one of her biscuits in half, passing some to her beloved Pug.
Irene giggled at the thought,
"Why don't you?" she asked, suddenly more animated than she had been in weeks.
"You could nominate him and I'll second the proposal."
"Don't be ridiculous." Maureen thought her friend had finally flipped, "He's a dog!"
"Exactly." Irene grinned, "But who would know?"
Maureen began to digest her friend's suggestion and a slow smile crept across her face.

"You're right, most of them don't know who lives in the flat next door, let alone who has a pet. It would show them all up for what they are," she mused, "and we could have a bit of fun at their expense."

Over a second cup of tea plans were made and anyone looking in on the scene would have wondered why two sixty-something women were giggling like school girls, decorum abandoned in their enthusiasm for a project to make a point to their neighbours.

Maureen gave a loud exaggerated cough to bring the meeting to order and then began.

"The main item on the agenda today is to elect a new chairman, a position which has been vacant since Mr. Goodbody sadly passed on. Nominations will be accepted during the next two weeks, when I suggest we re-convene to vote for a new leader." She looked at Irene and winked before continuing,

"I have one nomination to start the ball rolling. Mr Pinkerton at flat number 27 is happy to stand for election and I believe Irene here has agreed to second the motion." Maureen gazed around the room to see if anyone would connect the name to her flat number or her dog. The only noise was Irene, covering her face and clearing her throat in an attempt to stifle a giggle.

"Mr Pinkerton sends his apologies, he had wished to be here, but is otherwise tied up. Are there any other nominations?" The silence made her want to giggle, "Well in that case I suggest we attend to the next item on the agenda and discuss further nominations at the next meeting."

Maureen and Irene decided to treat themselves to lunch in town. It was an early celebration of what they were sure would be a victory for Mr. Pinkerton. They laughed at the absurdity of the whole situation and anticipated their fellow residents' reactions when they realised what their indifference had brought upon them.

At the next meeting Maureen again had to make apologies for Mr. Pinkerton's absence.
"He is sorry he cannot be here today, but I have a list of ideas he has been chewing over recently."
Neither woman was surprised that there were no other nominations. Irene chuckled and Maureen struggled to keep a straight face as she continued,
"Mr. Pinkerton has a keen nose for property matters. He promises to sniff out any problems before they become major issues." Maureen was encouraged by the nods and murmurs of approval from her audience.
"He is also very keen to keep up the maintenance of our communal gardens. He obviously derives much pleasure from this area and would like to make it suitable to spend more time in. Oh, and he also has several original ideas on dealing with the problem of the feral cats who seem intent on fouling our garden."
More encouraging noises almost persuaded Maureen herself that Mr. Pinkerton would be the ideal candidate for Chairman!
"May I also add that from my personal knowledge of Mr. Pinkerton, he is of impeccable character. By nature he is a genuine, easy going individual, altruistic in giving of his time and attention to others, seeking no material gain; an altogether ideal candidate. Therefore if there are no other nominations, I'm happy to propose that we elect Mr. Pinkerton as chairman of our residents' committee."
Irene raised her hand and spoke with confidence,
"I second the motion!"
Almost immediately every hand in the room was raised. Maureen had to bite her tongue to keep from laughing as she and Irene exchanged triumphant looks.

"Irene?" Madam Secretary asked, "Could you pop out to see if Mr. Pinkerton is free to join us now?"

As arranged beforehand, Irene made her way to Maureen's flat to collect an excited Mr. Pinkerton and take him to meet his very own committee. When they entered the room, Maureen tapped the table with her knuckles and announced.

"Ladies and gentlemen, I am delighted to introduce you to your newly elected chairman, Mr. Pinkerton!"

It took time for the committee to comprehend what was going on but slowly faces began to smile and laughter broke out as it dawned on them who Mr. Pinkerton was. Irene was delighted that their little plan had worked as she turned and whispered to Maureen, "Do you think they've got the point?"

The End

(Truth really is stranger than fiction. This scenario actually did happen in the US a few years ago.)

Underground

...he saw the jeweller on the floor with his open, unseeing eyes...

Carmel struggled to lift her baby, his pushchair and the shopping onto the train. Settling into the first available seat she began to relax, jiggling Majid on her knee hoping he would stay awake until they got home. She didn't often take him into the city; it was no place for a baby but today her childminder had let her down yet again. Still, they would be home in time for tea.

Sharon jumped onto the underground train effortlessly, swinging her lithe body into a window seat and smiling at the laughing baby in front. Plonking a bag determinedly on the seat beside her was an attempt to deter the greasy looking man from the platform who had been leering at her, from sitting next to her. Sharon's heart sank when he sat immediately behind and she felt his hand on the back of her seat, his fingers in contact with her blonde hair. Shifting position to thwart him, Sharon willed him to give up.

The carriage was relatively quiet. A grey suited business man, a nondescript middle aged lady and a forty-something young woman had entered from the other door and settled into their chosen seats. A sullen looking man whose deeply etched frown appeared to be a permanent feature, and a skinhead, displaying arms covered in tattoos, were the only other passengers.
The train hiccupped into motion; the occupants adopting that look of resignation which so often characterized regular underground users. Only the baby seemed excited

by the sudden movement and the prospect of the journey home.

Rattling along its well worn route, the train was about two minutes into a tunnel when the brakes were suddenly applied and it jerked to a halt. The abrupt stop was accompanied by a total blackout, which although only thirty seconds, seemed longer to the train's occupants. The baby's chuckles turned into a loud wail. When the lights began to flicker on, a sense of tension was almost tangible among the passengers. Eyes which had gazed blankly out of windows searched around for answers to the reason for this unscheduled stop.

Billy, the greasy looking man, leaned forward to Sharon.

"Nothing like a bit of excitement to liven things up eh? Could this be fate, throwing us together?" He touched her shoulder, uninvited. Shrugging him off, Sharon moved to sit with the middle aged lady who was looking rather tense at this unannounced stop.

"Hi", Sharon said, "That chap's giving me the creeps."

The woman attempted a smile,

"What's happening?" she asked, "Could it be a bomb d'you think?"

"Oh, something and nothing, I suppose, we'll get going again in a minute or two."

But the minute turned to four, then five. The lady began to rock backwards and forwards, mumbling under her breath.

"What's your name love?" Sharon asked to distract her.

"Moira.......sorry, I hate confined spaces. Why doesn't someone tell us what's happening?"

"Probably something technical; happens all the time." Sharon tried to keep her voice light-hearted to reassure her companion.

After fifteen minutes the other passengers were getting anxious too. Moira was having a panic attack and the man with the frown was becoming angry.

"Breathe slowly." Sharon suggested, "It won't be much longer I'm sure."

The baby began to cry again.

"Can't you shut him up?" Brian, the angry man, shouted.

"He's a baby." Carmel retaliated, maternal instinct rising to the fore, "He's hungry and shouting at him certainly won't help."

Brian scowled and moved away to the other end of the coach where the young skinhead had been trying his mobile phone.

"Any luck?" Brian asked.

"No signal." Mark replied absently.

"You'd think there'd be an announcement or something. What the hell's going on?"

Mark didn't respond. He was worried about the delay thinking about his brother, Sean and how he'd react if Mark was late; he wished he'd caught an earlier train.

Jane too looked worried, but remained seated, gazing into the blackness of the tunnel, transported back to the morning's conversation with her husband...

"Just remember what I told you last night. Don't even think about going out with those fancy friends of yours. Your place is here and you'll do as I say! Got that?" Frank knew she was afraid of him, but he had to hurt her occasionally just to remind her who was boss. He seemed to enjoy the power he held over his wife, and her fear excited him. Jane knew she must escape but was afraid, yet she could still think logically and had been making plans.

"It was only for coffee." Jane saw the anger rising in her husband, "But I'm not going out today, just doing the housework."

Frank snorted, turning back to the morning paper. As soon as he left for work, Jane had a quick tidy round, changed into her only decent outfit, walked to the tube station and caught the train into the city. The interview was early afternoon and hopefully wouldn't last too long; she desperately needed to be home before Frank. If he even suspected what she was doing....

James ran his finger around the neck of his shirt and loosened his tie, he was getting decidedly edgy. It was thirty minutes since the train stopped and no word as to why. Could they be onto him?

'Keep calm' he told himself, glancing at his reflection in the windows. A smart business man stared back, grey suit, short cropped hair; who would suspect anything? But why the stoppage? Were the police out there waiting to arrest him?

It should have been a simple job, quick and clean. James wasn't a seasoned criminal and this wasn't his first job, but it could be his last. The sales assistant had buzzed him into the shop without problem; these jewellers seemed to think a robber would be obvious; a mask, swag bag and stripey tee-shirt perhaps? But James looked like any of the other business executives who patronised such high class jewellers. Entry hadn't been the problem. The knife was only meant to scare the man, to control him into doing James's bidding; he had no intention of using it. Yes, the man was scared, that was the whole point but to have a heart attack or whatever, how could James have anticipated that? He felt pretty ill himself when he saw the chap laid on the floor, face as white as milk and eyes wide open, staring straight at him. Terrifying; he couldn't get out of there quick enough. And now this bloody train, what the hell was going on? Could he have been seen? Were the police waiting for him? Would they think he'd somehow killed the guy? He was having palpitations, sweat was pouring from him.

Carmel managed to get Majid to sleep so the only noise was Moira, softly crying and Sharon, trying to comfort her. Jane stood up and began to pace anxiously. Mark continued trying his mobile, a futile exercise which began to annoy Brian.
"Stop fiddling with that bloody thing can't you? If you couldn't get a signal before, you'll not get one now!"
Mark stood up; a tall gangly youth with broad shoulders and large hands. His close cropped hair and multiple tattoos made him appear hard. Moira flinched, thinking Mark was going to confront Brian, but the youth silently moved to the other end of the carriage.

Billy had given up on Sharon, deciding she was a stuck-up bitch. He turned his attention to Jane, whispering something as she walked past. A long, cold look left him in no doubt that his charms were wasted on her too. Maybe the flask in his pocket would offer more comfort.

James wiped his brow checking his watch again and pulling his briefcase closer, a feeling of nausea swept over him.

The loudspeaker crackled into life and as abruptly as it had stopped, the train lurched forward and a disembodied voice began an apology for the delay.

"Forty-five bloody minutes and that's the best they can do!" Brian ranted. "We should get compensation for this!"

The others ignored the outburst. Moira seemed able to breathe easier and Jane relaxed, the tension leaving her body. If there were no more delays and she hurried she could still make it home in time, then a couple more weeks and she'd be free....

The interview had gone well.

"You seem to have all the relevant experience and qualifications Mrs Henry," the manager had smiled, "So I'm pleased to offer you the position of senior housekeeper. As we discussed, the appointment starts on the first of next month, when the flat will available for you to move into."

She could have kissed him, but settled instead for a handshake, and now Jane allowed herself to dream about a new life. The hotel was everything she could want, a job in which to make her mark and feel valued for her efforts. The little flat would be her own personal haven, it couldn't come quickly enough and now that the train was moving again, Frank need never know she had been out.

Approaching their stop, Mark and James waited by the doors. Mark ran off as if his life depended on it, covering the mile to the day-care centre in record time. He could see his brother watching from the window, distressed, with tears flowing freely.

"You said you'd be here Mark!" he wailed.

"I'm here now Sean, I'm sorry buddy, the train was delayed and there was nothing I could do!" Mark felt terrible. His brother needed routine; it was part of his condition. Ever since their mother had died Mark had been Sean's carer and had never once been late to pick him up. He stroked Sean's head and his brother snuggled

into his neck. Sean was the elder but Mark had been thrust into playing the big-brother role, but he didn't mind or complain, Mark would do anything for him. As the sobs quieted, he looked into Sean's face.
"Guess I owe you a big mac to say sorry huh?" he asked.
Sean wiped his tear streaked face with his sleeve,
"With fries and a shake?" he grinned.

James told himself that the police couldn't possibly be onto him. The train had been delayed by an accident. He was filled with a desire to run but knew that would be stupid. Why draw attention when he was almost home and dry? Crazy thoughts flashed through his mind; he saw the jeweller on the floor with his open, unseeing eyes; he'd never seen a dead body before and knew he'd never forget it; it would almost certainly give him a few sleepless nights. He checked for security cameras, thinking that maybe the police had been following him on camera, like he'd seen on 'Spooks'. The breeze along the platform was welcome. He breathed deeply, focusing his mind.
'Walk slowly' he told himself, 'You're being paranoid!'
Suddenly, an angry voice from behind shouted. His blood ran cold but he kept moving, not daring to look back.
"Hey, you!" The voice was getting nearer.
'He's not shouting at me.' James told himself.
"Hey, mister, you with the grey suit!"
Should he make a run for it or try to bluff it out? Before he could decide he felt a strong grip on his arm.
"Are you deaf or something?" shouted the angry man. "You left your bloody briefcase, here, as if I haven't had enough hassle today."
James didn't know whether to laugh or cry. He couldn't believe he'd left his briefcase. It held the one thing he'd snatched before he ran, a diamond necklace which the jeweller had been cleaning; his only compensation for a

stressful day. James was beginning to realise that he needed a change of occupation. He squeezed the briefcase to his body as if it were a lover then turned towards the barrier but the smile which was forming on his lips was halted as he lifted his head and saw two uniformed policemen, looking sternly in his direction.

The End

Picture Perfect

"You never forget your first true love, and for me that was Adam Solomon" her grandmother had told her.

Amy had loved her grandmother dearly so naturally there was a huge gap left in her life when she died, but Lavinia had been ready to go. She'd had a long and happy life, not without its sadness, but she was a courageous, feisty lady who met challenges head on, counting her blessings with a smile and confronting her demons with a gritty determination which had sustained her throughout the years. Amy hoped she could emulate her Grandmother and although life was in many ways so much easier today, she was under no illusions that her way would be without complications.

Lavinia had lost her husband in the Second World War; they had married when they were both twenty-one and Amy's mother had been conceived in 1944, when the end of the war was in sight, an ending which hadn't come soon enough for Lavinia's young husband who had never returned to get to know his only child and consequent granddaughter. But Lavinia never complained; she had her daughter and a loving extended family and considered herself fortunate, rich in the things that really mattered. Amy often wondered why her grandmother had never remarried, even in her latter days she was still an attractive woman, sprightly to the end and always content with life.

As a child, Amy spent many happy hours with Lavinia, forming a bond of love which breached the generation gap with ease, nurturing a happy and relaxed relationship. Although Amy felt the loss of her grandmother keenly, there were many memories and a few treasures which

Gran had left her. By far the most cherished of these was an oil painting which had taken pride of place in her grandmother's little terraced home. It was a painting of a cottage, a single storey dwelling with whitewashed walls, reflecting the shadows and sunshine of the summer day on which the likeness was captured. The cottage was in the background, partially hidden by the riot of colour spilling over the garden. Amy could just pick out the pebbled pathway which was obscured with shrubs and flowers. Poppies, harebells, delphiniums and cornflowers competed for space on one side of the path, while a magnificent laburnum leaned over the other side, its branches weighed down with heavy clusters of brilliant yellow flowers. The artist had captured the garden at its best in the height of summer. Looking at it, you could almost smell the fragrance of the flowers, and the little blue gate painted in the foreground offered an open invitation to walk through and enjoy the delights of summer.

When she was sixteen, Amy asked her grandmother about the painting, wondering if it was a real home or just something conjured up from the artist's imagination.
"Oh, it's real enough." Gran answered. "I've been there plenty of times when I was a girl."
"Who was the painter Gran?" Amy asked, not entirely unaware of the distant, dreamy look on Lavinia's face.
"His name was Adam Solomon and he was the first man I ever loved."
Amy remained silent, willing her to continue. Gran had often spoken of her husband, but had never really talked about life before him. Lavinia sipped her tea and rewarded Amy's silence by continuing the tale.
"Adam and I grew up in the same village, Upper Walden, near Stroud. It was such a pretty place, I lived at the top end of the village and Adam lived at the bottom of the

hill in Pear Tree Cottage, that's it in the picture. He was such a talented boy, even in school we knew he'd go far. He could capture the very heart of a landscape and preserve it forever on canvas. And he was so good looking; all the girls swooned over him with his straw blonde hair and striking blue eyes. We were always friends but as we grew older, we became inseparable. I was no older than you are now and we were deeply in love." Lavinia seemed transported back to those teen years, Amy was anxious for her to continue.

"What happened to separate you Gran?"

"We were very young and when my father had to move to Norfolk to get work, Adam and I were devastated. Of course I had to go with my parents; their authority was unquestionable in those days. Adam gave me the painting as a parting gift although I needed nothing to remember him by and I've loved it ever since. We promised to keep in touch of course but then the war came along. Adam signed up as soon as he could and was sent abroad. I received one or two letters, but then we just lost touch. I met your grandfather a couple of years later and fell head over heels in love. You know the rest, but you never forget your first true love, and for me that was Adam Solomon. He was a good, kind man, but then so was your grandfather. I've been lucky to have loved two good men in my life, even if I didn't have either of them for as long as I might have wished."

Lavinia never spoke about Adam again but the story had been imprinted on the young Amy's mind and now, as she neared thirty, she no longer had her beloved Gran but did have a part of her life in Adam Solomon's beautiful painting.

Amy didn't know when the idea first came to her, but it took root until it became a fully formed plan. She would visit Upper Walden and find the cottage. Perhaps she would even find Adam Solomon, he could still be alive.

Appropriately, it was a glorious summer day when Amy set off on the pilgrimage to her grandmother's place of birth. She had carefully wrapped the precious painting in a blanket and wedged it in the boot of her Mini, unsure why she was taking it, but if she did find Adam, she would want to show him the painting. The journey was less than two hours by car but of course in Lavinia's day it would have seemed like the other side of the world.

Upper Walden was as pretty as Amy expected it to be. After a welcome coffee in the village pub, she left her car in the car park and set off to explore the village on foot. She knew her grandmother lived in one of the houses at the top of the village, although there was no way of finding out where, so Amy made her way to the bottom of the hill, where a handful of dwellings nestled in a chocolate box setting beside a stream. Locating the cottage proved to be easy and any problems she had anticipated were dispelled as she approached the bottom of the hill and was greeted by the familiar sight of a single storey, whitewashed cottage still with a blue gate and an amazing garden!

Stopping suddenly, Amy gasped, a strange feeling taking over her senses. The colours in the garden were the same, although perhaps a little more manicured than in the picture and the sun was still casting its shadows over the whitewashed walls. Amy felt a sense of belonging, as if she had arrived home. Should she go in? Her resolve was weakening; what if Adam was still alive, he may not remember his childhood sweetheart and that would be a bitter disappointment. Had she just been building up a silly, romantic picture?

As Amy dithered over her next move, the door of the cottage opened and a tall young man came out into the garden. He looked strangely familiar to Amy but she couldn't possibly have met him before.

'He must think I'm crazy' Amy thought, suddenly realising that she had been standing staring at the house for several minutes.

"Can I help you?" the young man asked, his cerulean eyes smiling from beneath a mop of straw blonde hair.

"I'm er... looking for someone who lived here a long time ago." She said, sounding unusually feeble. Amy prided herself on being strong and articulate, even feisty, as Lavinia had been.

"Do you have a name for this person?" The young man was smiling at Amy's embarrassment.

"Adam Solomon."

The man looked rather puzzled as he studied her with those piercing blue eyes.

"I'm Adam Solomon....I'm sorry, should I know you?"

Amy's mouth dropped open. Quickly closing it, her brain tried to work out what was happening here.

"But the gentleman I'm looking for is much older... could it perhaps be your father?" Even as she spoke the words, she knew that they were wrong; this man wasn't much older than herself.

"My father was James Solomon but my grandfather was Adam, could you be looking for him? Because if you are, I'm afraid he died five years ago."

"Oh, I'm so sorry." Amy was beginning to recover some of her usual composure, "Perhaps I should explain." It suddenly occurred to her why this man was familiar; he was the image of her grandmother's first love as Lavinia had described him and as Amy had pictured him in her mind.

Adam gestured to a bench in a shady spot of the garden. "Please, come in, you've aroused my curiosity now."
Sitting in the shade, beneath the laburnum tree, which she felt she had known all her life, Amy began to tell this young man all about Lavinia and the painting.
"My grandfather was a talented painter." Adam told her. "That's how I make my living too, although I don't think I'll ever be as good as my namesake!"
Amy wished she had brought the painting. She told Adam that it was in the car and he was eager to walk back to the pub so to see it and suggested they might have lunch there to continue their conversation. Amy was delighted at this offer, for some reason she wanted this day to continue without ever ending, and then scolded herself inwardly for being so childish.

Adam marvelled at the painting. He explained that there was very little of his grandfather's work left, it had nearly all been sold while he was alive, although he did have a few pencil sketches which he offered to show Amy after lunch.
Conversation flowed easily. Amy felt so comfortable with Adam as if she had known him all her life. She was however rather saddened that Adam had never heard his grandfather refer to Lavinia.
"He wasn't a great one for looking back. The war changed him and he held on to the belief that each day is precious and to be lived to the full. Perhaps that's what happens when you see your friends lost in battle?"

After lunch, they walked back down the hill to Pear Tree Cottage and went inside. It was everything Amy could have dreamed of. Original beams and an inglenook fireplace graced the cottage which had walls over a foot thick, creating beautiful deep window sills. Amy would have been disappointed had it been otherwise. Adam led the way through the house and into the rear garden, which proved to be just as exquisite as the front. There were two wizened old pear trees, still bearing fruit; Amy wondered if her grandmother had eaten the fruit from this tree and smelt the ripe pears as she could now. At the far end of the garden was a studio where, Adam explained, he did his painting. It was a wonderfully light and airy construction, with patio doors flung wide to let the sunshine flood the large open space.

"This wasn't here in grandfather's day," he told her, "I've added this; it's the perfect place to work in."

Amy had to agree, the room was delightful and when she saw Adam's paintings it was obvious he had been modest in saying that he wasn't as good as his grandfather. He too used oils as his preferred medium and although perhaps a little more contemporary in style, they were every bit as good as his namesake.

Adam left her to browse through the paintings while he searched for his grandfather's sketches among an assortment of old boxes in a cupboard.

"Here they are!" he said at last, unwrapping sheets of brown parcel paper which protected the old drawings and laying them out on the large work bench by the window. Amy could recognise his style in the landscape drawings, and there was even a pencil sketch of the cottage from the same vantage point as her painting. Perhaps this was the original sketch made in preparation for the oil painting, they would never know. Among the landscapes and a few seascapes, Adam pulled out a pen and ink drawing of a young girl. She was in profile with a wistful smile on her face and appeared to have not a care in the world. Amy smiled too, recognising the face of her grandmother. Adam's train of thought caught up with hers as he looked at the drawing and then at Amy.

"This is her isn't it? Your grandmother."

"Yes." Amy's voice was choked with emotion.
"L.M. That's all he put on this picture, but he kept it all this time."
"Lavinia Musgrove, my grandmother"
There was a warm satisfaction in knowing that Adam Solomon had not forgotten his first true love and had kept her portrait throughout his life. A few moments of silence were broken by Adam as he said,
"You look very like her, very beautiful."
Amy was lost in thought and hardly noticed the compliment. She eventually raised her eyes to meet Adam's gaze. Perhaps her grandmother's legacy would prove to be a priceless treasure after all, and in more ways than one!

The End

Say It With Flowers

I would have stepped into a bucket of water if he hadn't caught my arm to steady me!

Perhaps it was the daisy chains which prompted my ambition when I was the tender age of six. I remember spending many happy hours picking the fresh, simple flowers and carefully splitting the stalks to make the delicate chains for myself and my numerous dolls. If my mother or grandmother were around, I would even bestow one of my precious daisy chains on them, a gift with which they were naturally delighted. I think I decided even then that when I grew up I would sell flowers for a living.

I progressed from daisy chains to picking wild flowers and pressing them in between the pages of my father's thick medical books in his study. Each flower reminded me of where I had found it and I carefully looked up the names and filled several scrapbooks with my floral trophies. By the age of eleven, I was a walking encyclopaedia of botanical names!

In my teens I read about the language of flowers and how ancient civilizations had used them as expressions of emotions. Fascinating tales of Middle Eastern harems using flowers to send secret messages to lovers and stories of brave Roman soldiers being honoured with wreathes of laurels kept me enthralled. My love of flowers was fostered by my mother, an impassioned gardener and her father, Gramps, who virtually lived at his allotment. I was even christened Holly by my parents, more because I was a winter baby than a prickly child I hasten to add.

At fifteen, a work placement from school matched me with a florist and I thought I had died and gone to heaven. The wonderful scents from so many different blooms and the feast of colours everywhere I looked was ambrosia to my young heart and soul. My enthusiasm didn't go unnoticed and the florist offered me a Saturday job; what bliss.

My parents were remarkably supportive when I announced that I did not want to attend university. I know Dad had always hoped I would follow his example and go into medicine, but my heart was in flowers and my ambition was to own my own shop. After A levels, I began to work full time at the florists. I had so much experience that I was soon making up arrangements, even assisting with wedding flowers and funeral wreathes. I didn't mind the early mornings, in fact I loved the quiet peaceful time before opening when I could breathe in the fragrance of the flowers from the fresh deliveries, and prepare the day's displays.

The dream of my own florist shop became a reality after only three years in training. I had won a few competitions and was building a good reputation with our customers, many of whom requested my work for special orders. My parents helped financially and I became the proud owner of a small outlet, hardly more than a glorified closet really, situated in a busy arcade, with great opportunities for passing trade. Life was wonderful. I didn't care about the long hours and the fact that I was working on my own; there were regular customers who came in for a chat when it was quiet and always something to do in my workroom at the back of the shop. Mum would occasionally take over for a half day to give me a break. I think she worried about my long hours more than I did, wanting me to have a social life and meet people. (That's mother talk for "It's time you had a boyfriend!")

But I was meeting people; there were the regular business men who came in each Friday to buy flowers for their wives, embarrassed young men wanting bouquets to impress their girlfriends and children looking for flowers for their mothers. Trade was seasonal, always something to look forward to and plan for; valentine sprays, inexpensive posies for mother's day, summer weddings, Christmas arrangements, what variety. I loved my work and never felt lonely, how could I with a shop full of fragrant flowers to keep me company?

Harry first entered the shop in late summer. I had just completed a new display, dahlias and chrysanthemums in rich velvety colours surrounding a little water feature I had found at the garden centre, exactly the right size for my limited space. I nearly toppled into his arms as I tried to extricate myself from the jungle of greenery waiting to be sorted and would have stepped into a bucket of water had he not caught my arm to steady me. Blushing and apologising, I asked if I could help. He in turn blushed too, embarrassed to reveal that he was unsure which flowers to choose.
"They're for a colleague...well, a lady, more than a colleague I hope. We're just friends... at the moment that is, but, well you know I'd like to get to know her a little better."
"Yes, I see... so you want something that's not over the top, but will let her know you like her?" I enquired.
"Exactly! Not red roses, they mean true love don't they? Something a little less than that at this stage." He looked directly at me and I was aware of how close he was standing, and how the colour was rising in my cheeks again.

"How about red carnations?" I offered, "They speak of admiration rather than passion, and perhaps some baby's breath to go with them, a symbol of happiness."

"Admiration and happiness, perfect, thank you." He smiled.

Another satisfied customer and a lucky girl too, I thought as I made up the spray, gathering the blooms with matching red ribbon.

Over the next couple of days I wondered how the carnations had been received and what kind of a girl the object of Harry's devotion was but it was over a fortnight before I saw him again. "Did she like the flowers?" I ventured

"Oh yes, thank you, but to tell the truth, I don't feel I'm any further forward. I wondered about something which says a little more?"

"I've got some beautiful alstromeria fresh in today. They speak of devotion and friendship. They last well too."

Harry seemed pleased with the alstromeria and bought twenty stems. Whoever the lady was she must be pretty special. I couldn't help noticing those soft brown eyes and his slightly crooked smile, which made him look like an endearing puppy.

The next time I saw Harry, the smile was gone. He waited as I served a customer.

"Can I ask you something?" he looked solemn.

"Of course." I tried to be chirpy.

"It's a bit embarrassing really. I've never been very good at talking to girls. You're different, you remind me of my little sister. Anyway this girl at work...I don't seem to be getting anywhere. What would you suggest?"

My initial reaction was to say, forget her, take me out instead and the thought shocked me even as it was forming in my mind. I made an effort to be professional,

"Perhaps you could give more of a hint." I advised. "How about gardenia? They say, 'You're lovely' and speak of secret love."

Harry nodded, he had picked up a stem of eucalyptus and was staring at it thoughtfully.

"Eucalyptus means protection. Shall I add some to the gardenia?"

He paid for the flowers and left.

I am ashamed to say that I hoped the object of Harry's desire suffered from hay fever! I couldn't stop thinking about him, his face was with me day and night and I wanted to be the one to bring that smile back again. I wondered how it would feel to have him give me flowers and be infatuated with me, but that was never going to happen was it?

It was late autumn before I saw Harry again. That was the day I learnt his name, and I remember thinking how it suited him. Once more he hovered until there were no other customers in the shop.

"I'm sorry to bother you again," he began "But I could do with your advice. She seems to appreciate the flowers, but other than a brief thank you I'm getting no-where, is there anything else you could suggest?"

I asked him then, even though I didn't really want to know, or did I?

"What's she like... I mean it's difficult to suggest flowers for someone I don't know."

"Yes of course, sorry. Well, she's very beautiful, everyone thinks so, tall and slim and always immaculately turned out. Just about perfect really."

I asked for that one didn't I? I was suddenly very conscious of my short, pear shaped figure and tried to hide my hands, there were bits of oasis stuck in my fingernails from earlier. I bet she never had grubby hands!

"An orchid, a single orchid" I said, "Or calla lilies. They speak of beauty and love."

Harry was looking strangely at me.

"Yes, fine," he said watching as I moved over to the lilies. "And where would you take her at this time of year? Somewhere out of the office, I never see her outside the office."

Now I was feeling decidedly grumpy.

"Well, my idea of a good day out at this time of year is to wrap up well and take my dog for a long walk in the country, stopping for a plough man's at a village pub!"

"You have a dog?" There was that smile again. Couldn't he see that thinking of her only worried him?

"I have a dog too, a border collie called Tess."

Well, the shop was quiet; I could always catch up after closing. We talked, really talked for the first time, and he was every bit as gorgeous as I had imagined. He formally introduced himself offering me his hand, and I felt goose bumps run through my body. We chatted for ages and had so much in common it was incredible. I felt deflated when he had to leave, taking the lilies for 'her'.

Christmas was approaching, my third as an independent florist and my favourite time of year. The usual scent of the flowers was spiced up with that special Christmas smell. I went into work early to make up holly wreathes which were flying off the shelves as soon as I made them. At the beginning of each day I would line up the poinsettias at the doorway and marvel at how quickly I sold out. Their message of good cheer is perfect for the festive season. I had prepared hyacinths in September and they were now just beginning to flower, their distinctive scent filling the shop. Groups of children came from the local schools to sing carols in the arcade, adding to the atmosphere as shoppers hurried around like whirling dervishes, bags spilling over with food and gifts.

It was a few weeks since I had seen Harry. I wondered if Ms Perfect had taken him up on that date; she would be a fool not to. Still, I hoped in my heart that things hadn't worked out, then felt deservedly guilty for such mean thoughts. Harry was a lovely man who deserved to be happy, and she was probably a lovely person too.

The weather was pretty cold with frosty mornings and low temperatures all day. I was wrapped up like an Eskimo, the wind whipped through the arcade and a few extra layers were in order. I could do nothing about my permanently red nose; the cold always pinches my nose first. Between groups of carollers, piped music played festive songs. I enjoy music, but I was just having a grumble to one of my regulars, saying how I would scream if I heard Slade singing 'I wish it could be Christmas every day' again, when Harry walked in. My heart jumped into my throat and I'm sure my cheeks matched my nose.

"Hello!" he said when the customer had gone.

"Hi," I responded weakly, "How are you?"

If he had come to buy 'her' red roses, my Christmas would be ruined. My goodwill to all men did not extent to Ms Perfect!

"The shop looks good." He remarked.

"Thanks, Christmas displays are always the best to do." Oh, how pathetic I sounded.

"Can I get you anything?" It was nearly closing time and the shoppers were leaving the arcade. Harry looked directly into my eyes.

"It didn't work out." He blurted, "She doesn't like flowers and worse than that, she doesn't like dogs! When I eventually plucked up the courage to ask her out for a country walk and pub lunch, she laughed and asked if I was serious."

"I'm so sorry..." I began

"I'm not," Harry smiled his crooked smile. "I couldn't stop thinking about you. It was you I really wanted to share the country walk with, you and your talk of flowers, you with your unruly hair and the scent of this shop around you."

I was speechless. Harry picked up a sprig of mistletoe and twirled it in his fingers.

"I don't need to ask what this is for!" He smiled, and his kiss was just as wonderful as I had imagined it would be.

The End

Old Friends

*What he had taken for a bundle of rags
suddenly began to move!*

Andy ducked into the shop doorway just in time as the drizzle turned into torrential rain. The crack of thunder made him shudder and the following lightening suddenly illuminated the doorway revealing that he was not alone. What he had taken for a bundle of rags suddenly began to move and the gaunt figure of a man stood up to face him with a hard stare from cold dark eyes. Andy shrugged the droplets from his Armani suit and pretended the other man didn't exist. He couldn't escape from the doorway unless he was prepared to get drenched to the bone.

"I know you." The tramp's voice was raspy and flat, without inflection or emotion. "But I bet you don't remember me."

Andy blinked, squinting to try and see clearly through the gloomy winter's evening. A street lamp cast the only light; all the shops were in darkness, customers and staff long gone, home to a warm house and a hot meal he imagined. The tramp was about his own height and build but he could make out very little else. His lower face was covered by a dirty, matted beard and eyes obscured by long damp tresses of greasy hair. The tramp, he thought, could certainly benefit from a good hot bath, Andy was beginning to feel nauseous from the smell of dirty clothes, alcohol and body odour. It was impossible to guess the man's age but he was certain they had never met.

"I think you've got the wrong man pal." Andy turned away to look again at the rain, hoping it had eased but if anything it was even heavier.

"Andy Patterson, United's best leftie since the nineteen eighties." Of course the tramp would recognize him; his photo was always in the papers for one reason or another, documenting his prowess on the field and his antics off it too. The price of being a celebrity. Andy gave a forced smile, after all a fan is a fan. He began fishing in his pocket to give him one of the signed photos he carried around with him and perhaps he'd give the old boy a tenner too, make his night for him.

"We played together on St. William's School under fifteens, and after that we went on to the local youth team, remember? Good mates we were in those days, we dreamed big and played hard."

Andy peered at the tramp trying to see past the disgusting beard and the layers of filthy clothes.

"Ben? Ben Robson, it can't be, surely not..." Andy was astounded.

"Yeah, it's me. Surprised you remember now you're such a big shot. I thought we were friends once. You were the brother I'd always wanted, but I was expendable wasn't I, just like Sally? Ever think of Sal do you, my baby sister? You finished my career and ruined her life all in the same year, then left us both high and dry when you went off to be the next Wayne Rooney. Didn't want to know Sal when she got pregnant did you? Sent your 'agent' to take care of it. Money is always the answer isn't it?"

"Now hang on a minute, we were just kids! A baby would have been equally as bad for her as it would have been for me, it was the best solution all round."

"So your agent said. But you could forget; Sally couldn't. She was devastated, never trusted anyone again after that. The abortion ruined her. She's a mess, granted not in the same way as me, but a mess all the same."

"You can't pin that on me! Look at yourself, what example have you been to her? Having a brother like you is more than likely the cause of any problems Sally has."

"True, I'll give you that, but how do you think I got to be like this. Memory failing you is it? Let me remind you. It was that so called friendly game at the beginning of the season. We were both in line to be signed up for United's youth team; my talent was every bit as good as yours but I was 'loaned out' to the opposing side for that match, remember, they were a man down?"

Andy did remember, all too well. If the light had been better the tramp would have seen the colour draining from his face. The guilt and shame of what he had done had been pushed to the back of his mind only troubling him on rare occasions and soon forgotten with a couple of drinks under his belt. He'd twisted the facts so many times that he himself had begun to believe that he had no culpability in Ben's accident. The tramp continued in his emotionless flat voice.

"You had to show off didn't you? Your image was more important than fair play. I was your friend but you were determined to ruin me, to have all the glory for yourself."

"Now hang on a minute..." Andy interrupted. "It was a legitimate tackle; I couldn't have known what would happen."

The tramp didn't speak for a full minute, leaving Andy's words hanging in the air, both men recognizing the lie.

"You weren't going for the ball were you? Your kick was aimed directly at me. Did you hear the bone crack? I did, I can still hear it in my sleep sometimes. I was the best player on that field and you wanted me off so you could shine. Well you succeeded, you got me off, permanently. I've never played again, but you wouldn't know that would you? You left while I was still in hospital. Why was it you never came to visit? We were friends weren't we? But I was expendable, someone to trample over on your way to the top."

Andy was trembling at the tramp's words. He wanted to turn away and hurry back to his penthouse flat and his cosy life but for some reason he couldn't move, he was frozen to the spot feeling the cold seeping through to his bones. He wanted to defend himself but couldn't find the words. Shame and humiliation had taken hold of him, he wanted to apologize but that would be admitting his guilt. What did this tramp want? Why couldn't he just turn and run for home?

"I remember the pain, the agony of the injury and the knowledge that I'd never play again. Did you care Andy? Did you ever for one moment regret what you had done?"

Andy's discomfort was growing with every word. He had to try to put his slant on it.

"Now hang on a minute, I think you're getting things way out of proportion here. Accidents happen, its fate, bad luck if you like, I had...."

"You had what? A glamorous career ahead of you, money to burn, girls to fawn over you, cars, property? How much is it you earn each week, sixty, eighty, a hundred grand? That's more than most people get in a lifetime."

"A footballer's career is short, you know that, the money's relative."

"It's obscene!"

"Who are you to judge? I don't have to justify myself to you, look at you, a filthy dirty tramp, a drunken bum. You're hardly in a position to criticize others."

The tramp was still again, watching the angry tirade with his blank stare. A slow smile began to form on his lips.

The light from the street lamp reflected from Andy's Rolex as he waved his arms around in exasperation. He quickly pulled his sleeve down, embarrassed by the ostentatious possession.

His anger was spent. He did not know what to do so reached into his pocket changing to a more conciliatory tone.

"Look Ben, let's not let this get out of proportion." He unrolled a wad of twenty pound notes, beginning to peel some off. Ben's anger rose to the surface again,
"Don't you dare try to salve your conscience with money. I don't want your filthy lucre!"
"It's a gift, just a token, a little something to help you along. Take it, please."
There was a piercing feral scream like the cry of a wild animal. Andy took a moment to realise it was coming from the tramp who threw himself at Andy, knocking him against the plate glass window of the shop. Andy thought it would shatter with the force, but it didn't. He slid down to the wet pavement feeling vulnerable and afraid as Ben towered over him. The sickly smell of filth filled his nostrils and he turned his head shielding his face with his arms, fearful of what was about to happen. With another loud cry, the tramp stamped with both feet onto Andy's legs, the swift movement powered by years of repressed anger, his aim as true as the talented striker he had once been. This time they both heard the cracking of bone and as Andy passed out with the pain, the tramp moved quietly away feeling for the first time in many years that justice had at last been served.

The End

The Lift
She reminded me of my Granny, silver grey hair in a plaited bun and knitting needles poking out of an oversized handbag.

An occasional night of luxury is the perfect antidote to the pressures of modern living and as I soaked in the Jacuzzi bath trying all those complementary little bottles of shampoo and body wash, I resolved to do it more often. I worked hard and deserved such little treats. The hotel room was a dream; king sized bed with satin sheets, TV, mini bar, and a view to die for. Wrapping myself in the thick white towels I was grateful for the air conditioning as temperatures outside soared to record highs. But reality beckoned and I had to get back out there to earn my living.

I like to dress soberly when I'm working, not wanting to draw attention to myself, so I left off the party clothes from the night before and prepared for my working day. A charcoal grey suit, not too short, with my hair scraped back and twisted into a knot held in place with clips and just the slightest hint of make-up. I grabbed my bulky shoulder bag and was ready to face the day.

Stepping out of the room was like opening an oven door, the heat engulfed me immediately. The windowless corridors were stuffy and airless, but I'd soon be out of here and it would probably be a long time before I returned to this particular hotel. As I waited for the lift, (eighteen floors up is really too much for the stairs, even going down), a young man in a suit came along with his eyes firmly locked onto his mobile phone. He stopped beside me but there was no eye contact as we waited in silence. The lift seemed to take eons and when it eventually arrived there was just enough room for mobile man and myself to squeeze in.

I worked my way to the back wall as the other passengers shifted positions to make room for us. The heat in the lift was stifling with pungent smells of cologne and body odour mingling together, I sighed and waited. Directly in front of me was a balding man with one of those thin, straggly ponytails which only served to make him look ridiculous, hanging over his suit collar. I was seized by a sudden urge to cut it off and was grateful that I had no scissors in my bag. He was probably approaching sixty with his middle aged spread sitting firmly in all the wrong places and a sheen of perspiration threatening to run off his bald pate. The other occupants of the lift were a large, rather loud American lady and her husband. She was fixated about the diabolical service at the evening meal the previous night. There was another older business man with a pin stripe suit and the obligatory briefcase, which was most likely only used for his sandwiches. We were all heading for the ground floor where we would scurry off to our daily duties, most likely never to see each other again. The American lady continued her diatribe on poor service, her husband nodding in what he probably hoped to be the right places. They reminded me of one of those old sea-side postcards of the fat lady with the scrawny little husband wearing his knotted hankie on his head, although she certainly didn't look as if she would approve of him wearing such casual attire.

The Lift suddenly jerked and ground to a halt, accompanied by a grating, mechanical noise which made me wince, like finger nails on a blackboard used to at school. When the doors didn't open it became obvious that we were in between floors, and there was a problem.
"Well. This is just typical!" the American lady, who was dressed as loudly as she spoke, drawled. All the occupants began to look around, as if the answer to why the lift had stopped would be written on the walls. One or two little

shuffles suggested the anxiety that some of the occupants felt, but apart from our cousin from across the pond, we all remained silent.

Mobile man didn't flinch. He was busy texting as if his life depended on it. A few years ago he would have been described as a yuppie, designer labels on every item of clothing and the Rolex watch to show the world that he was upwardly mobile. The other business man unfolded his copy of the Times and began to read. I had been standing behind the ponytail long enough, so I edged along the back wall until I was next to Mr and Mrs USA. The lift was less than two metres square, and by the time we had been stationary for four minutes, the heat was getting to us all. I moved on from the couple and weaved my way behind the pin striped suit. He was still reading having only lifted his head once, to remark knowledgably that this sort of thing occurred frequently and the lift would soon be on the move. Ah... the comforting voice of experience.

The smell of recycled garlic from the pin striped suit was getting to me, so I moved on again to a spot between mobile man and the pony tail; I had almost completed a full circle. After five minutes, which took several hours to pass, the grinding mechanical noise was to be heard again, coupled with a few more jerking movements and then the lift was back on track, arriving at the ground floor much to the relief of all the occupants.

When the doors opened, the American lady steered her husband towards reception to lodge her growing list of complaints. The other three of my travelling companions headed towards the dining room, no doubt to sample the full English breakfast on offer. And me? I turned to go in the direction of the concierge's office. Well, I say office, although it's more of a cupboard really, behind reception, but it gives him the status he thinks he deserves. I was just thinking that my working day was coming quickly to an end when my progress was halted by a little old lady in the reception area. She had the look of a sweet Miss Marple type, (but hopefully without the perceptive mind,) and was obviously struggling with an assortment of bags and a lumpy old suitcase. She reminded me of my Granny, silver grey hair in a plaited bun and knitting needles poking out of her oversized handbag.

"Excuse me dear." Her dulcet, southern counties accent was barely audible. "Do you think you could help me into the lift, the porters are all so busy?"

How could I refuse?

"Thank you my dear, you're so kind, I can always tell from the face and yours is such a pretty, honest face. I pride myself on being a good judge of character." She held onto my arm for support.

As I placed her bags inside the lift, I smiled and pressed the floor number for her and as the doors closed her periwinkle blue eyes held mine for an instant, then she was gone and I was left, still smiling. I turned back towards the concierge's office with a sigh and tapped lightly on the door.

"Hi Tony!" I beam at him. "Great timing today, spot on. I managed to get round all the occupants in the five minutes you gave me. Three wallets, nice fat ones too, a Rolex, a couple of credit cards and a crocodile purse, no doubt stuffed full of lovely dollars. Not a bad day's work eh? Pretty good hourly rate there don't you think?"

He began to sort through my day's 'takings' nodding his approval, while telling me,

"Good girl, but you'll have to leave this hotel off your list for a while, the maintenance men are getting suspicious. My old pal Jimmy, the concierge at The Maple Leaf says you could go back there again and I've a couple of new hotels you could add to your list..."

Tony's eyes widened and his mouth dropped open as I pulled out the last thing I had procured that day, a magnificent Cartier diamond bracelet courtesy of Miss Marple.
"What on earth..." he gasped.
I grinned at him, sharing his pleasure, it must have been one of the best items we had ever had.
"Just a little overtime bonus Tony!"

The End

True Identity

Her father would stop whatever he was doing, lift her up onto his knee and for the next hour or so they would be transported to the magical world of her story books.

Kate had turned forty-two before finding out her true identity. It happened on a bright spring morning when the warmth of the sun's rays brought a feeling of hope and new beginnings after a long bleak winter. It was a winter which had robbed Kate of her adored father and now she faced the daunting task of sorting through her parents' house in preparation for going on the market. As an only child, the house and its contents were left entirely to Kate whose mother had died ten years previously and for the last decade father and daughter had grown closer than ever. George White would be greatly missed by Kate and her husband Rob, and by their children, James and Lucy who had idolized their grandfather.

Walking down the path to the front door, Kate chided herself for not starting the task sooner. Leaves had blown into the lobby and the garden had taken on an uncared for look which would never have happened while her parents were alive. Turning the key in the lock she shivered, not remembering ever having entered the house whilst empty since before her wedding and now it seemed to have taken on a cold, unwelcoming atmosphere. Kate went through each room opening windows to let the sun in, to warm and freshen the house, before deciding to tackle the paperwork first. There were still people to inform about her father's death and what seemed like a mountain of papers to be sorted through, an altogether daunting prospect.

The study on the first floor had always been her father's exclusive domain. As a child it was a special treat to be allowed inside, and in later years her father had found comfort sitting in here with his memories and books. Kate's father had been an English professor at the university and the study reflected a passion for literature. One wall was completely covered in books, his pride and joy, although gathering dust now. Sitting in the big leather chair, Kate could almost feel her father's presence. The room smelled of his cologne and the pipe he used to smoke in here, much to her mother's disgust. Looking around she experienced a mixture of emotions, sadness, yes, but also contentment. Her father had had a long and happy life, which was never quite the same after he lost his wife; he had grown weary and was ready to join her. Kate understood, and in some small way it eased her sorrow.

The large metal box where they had kept their important documents was the first thing Kate needed to see. As well as all the financial papers and the deeds of the house, she came across her parents' birth certificates and their marriage certificate. The temptation to reminisce, especially when finding a pile of old photographs, was strong and she had to be firm in keeping on task, otherwise the time would be lost and she really didn't have the luxury of wasting time. Getting to the bottom of the papers, she unfolded another birth certificate, and this was the moment her world was suddenly thrown completely off balance.

The date of birth she was looking at was hers, but the name was not and the parents' names were not George and Annie White. Kate's mind began to work at speed, later when telling Rob, she acknowledged that from the first moment of reading the certificate she had known what it meant, but her brain was engaged in eagerly trying to find some other logical explanation. Kate did not want to admit that this document revealed that she was in fact, not her parents' natural child as she had always believed, but the child of a woman whose name she had never heard and she was not Kathryn White either.

A sudden chill gripped her, seeping right through to the bone in spite of the warm spring sunshine wafting through the open window. Kate could not move from the chair she was sitting in... her father's chair... but he was no longer her father and never had been.

How much time elapsed before she moved, Kate couldn't say. It was as if in a vacuum, time stood still, and she was suddenly very afraid. The birth certificate became blotted with tears, then suddenly she thrust it back into the box and ran around the house closing the windows before escaping into the warm fresh air outside.

"I don't want to go back there ever again!" Kate sobbed to her husband that evening.

"Well of course, you don't have to if you can't face it, but that will mean I'll have to do the clearing out and I don't want to make those kinds of decisions for you."

Rob had been very sympathetic when his wife told him of her discovery, not fully understanding the impact this had had on his wife. To him, George and Annie had been wonderful parents and people he had always admired, what did it matter who had actually given birth to her? But the weekend was filled with Kate's angst as she swung between a deep sadness and then a bitter anger at her parents for keeping this huge secret. Rob did his best to cheer her up, but felt he was failing miserably and at a loss to know what to do.

The following week passed in much the same way. Kate returned to work, but her mind was far away. Unable to explain those intrusive feelings, she no longer knew who she was, feeling somehow like an outsider looking in on her own life and still harbouring anger at her parents for not having told her about her origins. There had been times at school as a girl when they had looked at family trees and Kate could clearly remember her father talking about his parents, her 'grandparents'. It had all been a lie, how could such honest, decent people live a lie like that?

As the weekend approached, Rob told his wife that he intended to go to her parents' house to do some work on the garden which had been sadly neglected of late.
"I'm taking James and Lucy," he announced, "They're old enough to help and there's such a lot to do." He didn't push Kate into going, just asked for some sandwiches to take so they could stay all day and hopefully get most of the work finished. Kate waved them off, unsure how to fill the day without her family. Yes, there was always the housework, but she wasn't really in the mood. By mid day, Kate was feeling frustrated, she missed having Rob and the children around, weekends was their family time, and it was hard to do anything constructive on her own. After some internal arguments, her practical nature won the day and grabbing the car keys she jumped into her car, setting off to join her family.

Kate let herself in, moving through the quiet house cautiously as if she might disturb some memory and be confronted with her past. Entering the dining room she could see through the French windows where Rob and the children sat on the newly mown lawn, eating their sandwiches. Looking at the back of Lucy's head, it could have been herself thirty years ago. There had been dozens of picnics on that lawn with her parents and toys; tea parties for which her mother would always find some little treat to eat, iced gems, her favourite, or pink and white marshmallows. Kate couldn't help but smile at the memory. James caught sight of his mother and waved as she opened the door to go out and join them.

Rob's pleasure was obvious. His grin was infectious and Kate found herself returning his smile for almost the first time since making her discovery. After admiring the efforts made in the garden, she left them to continue and once again made her way tentatively to the study.

Opening the door released that familiar scent, evoking memories of long ago. As a child, this room had seemed like an enchanted grotto. On those special occasions when she'd been invited in, Kate had taken some of her picture books for her father to read. He would stop whatever he was doing, lift her up onto his knee and for the next hour or so they would be transported to the magical world of story books. How she'd loved those times. A quiet hour with a book was still a favourite pastime today, a legacy from George White which would always be with her. Kate sat once more in the faded leather chair. Scanning the shelves full of books, her eyes caught the beautifully bound red notebooks in which her father always seemed to be scribbling. Rising from the chair, Kate moved over to blow the dust from the top of the books. Her mother would never have let this room become so neglected. Opening the first one, Kate realised they were journals. How typical of a man who loved the written word to have kept a journal. The more faded volumes were from her father's youth, tales of a happy childhood written in a young boy's hand. The books were chronologically ordered and selecting a few to browse, Kate felt a sense of guilt, of being intrusive, yet at the same time, a strong desire to learn more about this man she had thought to be her father.

Kate read accounts of her parents' courtship, the writing was such a romantic style it hardly seemed the work of a young man. Their marriage at the tender age of eighteen brought such happiness, but as Kate skipped through the years it was obvious that the marriage was not complete and that their heart's desire was for a child. She began to read,

"My darling Annie was again brought to tears this morning as it was once more made clear that there was no baby to look forward to. Fifteen years we have been wed and our union has never been blessed with the child we both long for. I pray each night that this miracle will happen, but hope is dashed so easily..."

Kate's eyes filled with tears, picturing George and Annie in their youth; she had seen many photographs of this handsome couple. How sad her father had sounded. George hadn't written in his journal every day, but there were jottings and anecdotes at least once a week. She moved on to the year before she was born.

"Our marriage is almost certainly never to be blessed with a child. The doctors have found no reason, be we have accepted it as God's will. It is not easy, especially for my dearest Annie, who, if ever a woman was born to be a mother, she is that woman. But we do not despair. Today we have made enquiries into adopting a child. It seems that there are many children born to those who cannot, for some reason or other, look after them. Is this to be our destiny? We will persevere and find out if this path is right for us."

Kate's tears were flowing freely now. She found the journal dated nearly a year later.

"Our prayers have been answered! After months of examinations of our characters, classes on parenthood and interviews we have today been told that there is a baby girl, just three weeks old, who is to be ours if we want her. Of course we want her, we can't wait to see her

and bring her home, but we have to move slowly while the paperwork is sorted out. What joy! I could sing from the roof tops, a baby girl..."

Wiping her eyes, Kate fumbled through the pages of the journal until finding what she was looking for.

"Today is the most wonderful day of our lives! We have a baby daughter. Her given name is Pamela, but we have decided to change it to Kathryn, she will be Kate, our beautiful little girl. Annie is radiant, I haven't seen her look so happy for years, and she is already a wonderful mother, so natural. I however feel clumsy; I think I might drop her or squeeze her too hard, I love her so much! Annie tells me to be confident, she's not made of china, but to me she's just like a little doll, my precious Kate!"

This was almost too much to take in. For the last week she had been feeling lost and alone, thinking only about the woman who had given her away and assuming that for whatever reason she was unwanted. Now to read her father's own words, his expressions of joy at having her, everything was turned around again. Kate thumbed through the journals; the thread was the same, she was George and Annie's world.

As if in answer to the question at the back of her mind, 'Why didn't they tell me?' an entry after her mother's death shed a little light of understanding.

"It is several weeks now since my beloved Annie departed. How lonely I feel. If it wasn't for Kate, I wouldn't be able to go on. She is such a wonderful daughter, and strangely has grown to be more like Annie in nature as a daughter can be. I kept my promise to Annie, never to tell Kate that she is not our natural daughter. Annie was afraid that we would lose her; that she may go off on a quest to find her birth mother. She could never take that risk, but now the decision is mine to make alone. I will take my time. Perhaps it is too late, goodness knows it has been hard concealing it at times; I

have had to be quite inventive to keep this secret. Now we shall see what life brings. If the opportunity comes, who knows? But she will always be my Kate, my beautiful daughter.

Rob quietly entered the study as Kate was reading her father's words. She reached up for him and he held her while she sobbed. Pulling away after several minutes, she smiled at her husband.
"I understand all I need to know now." She told him. "The opportunity for him to tell me in life never came, but he's told me all I need to know now, and yes, I do understand. I just hope I can be as good a parent as mine have been for me."
Rob and Kate went down to find their children. It was time to go home. Kate would read the rest of the journals in due course, and through them she would find out who she really was and more about those remarkable people who chose to be her parents.

The End

I Wish...

...I will cherish my two men.

I smooth my hands over my heavy, swollen belly, smiling at the thought of this precious new life growing within. An elbow, or perhaps a foot, juts out at the side and I gently massage my baby, willing him to know and feel my love. Each movement is a delight, a miracle comparable to none other. Just a few more weeks now; time for him to grow a little stronger and be ready to face the world, announcing his presence with a cry.

I wish for him a good life, happiness more than wealth, love more than hate, friends and family to cherish. I wish him sunshine and soft breezes, rainbows which never end, rich green grass and clear blue skies. I wish him warmth and comfort, a peaceful path to walk and good health.

The ache in my back is no trouble; the stretch marks across my growing stomach are a delight, a badge to wear with pride proclaiming my new found status as a mother. He will be called Matthew after his father and I will cherish my two men.

Labour is certainly the right word for giving birth, an indescribable blend of the very best and the worst. My darling boy has arrived, so perfect, with his father's red hair. Matthew and I are now parents, a true family at last, ready to face the world together.

My beautiful baby is certainly getting his share of attention. The doctors do so many tests; my poor boy is woken to have blood taken and his limbs moved around. Can't they see he's perfect?

Down's syndrome they whisper, but I already know. I have seen those children with round, laughing faces and almond shaped eyes, who grow, yet never grow up, still holding their parent's hands as adults.

They say we're in denial that we haven't accepted his 'disability', but I say it's they who are in denial. We love our son; he is special and will bring us joy and pain as all children do. We will watch him grow and marvel at each little accomplishment.
Matthew sleeps so peacefully, his little rosebud mouth damp, his soft eyelashes resting on his plump little cheeks. We loved him before he was born and now as we are getting to know him we love him even more.
He is and will always be our beautiful boy!

The End

One Step at a Time

I thought at one point that a tiny smile quivered on his lips, but it could have been wishful thinking!

It wasn't the sort of decision to be made lightly, it would mean a complete change in lifestyle and my husband and I knew that we'd have to be totally committed; to make this decision and then renege on it could have catastrophic consequences, but it was a scary undertaking.

Our precious children were grown up, Sam, in his third year at university and Emma, our eldest was now a mother herself, enjoying her new found status to the full, as indeed I was as a novice grandma. So, in theory, life could be taken more easily with the time to indulge in new hobbies, to travel, whatever we liked really. But that was the problem; we weren't quite ready for the slowing down stage. Having begun our family early, we still felt young ourselves, relatively speaking of course. We'd always thrived on the busyness of family life, enjoying the ups and downs, making the most of each magical stage of our children's growth and development, which had seemed to pass as swiftly as the seasons of the year. Still feeling there was more to give, and having been blessed with so many of life's good things, we wanted to share our good fortune. I'm not talking about financially; we had always been comfortable in monetary terms, though not rich! But we had a home and, more importantly, love, and it was that love we wanted to share.

Emma was the one who first suggested fostering. Although on maternity leave now, her job was with the local authority children's services and she knew of the desperate need for foster carers.

"You and Dad would be brilliant Mum, you're made for the role, I can vouch for that."
"I don't think you would have felt that way when you were a teenager." I reminded her laughing.
"Yes, well, the least said about that the better," my daughter grinned back at me. We'd had the usual family problems, struggling with adolescence as much as any parent, which is why we thought long and hard before embarking on fostering a child. Having heard some of the horror stories from Emma, we had anything but a rosy picture of what we could be letting ourselves in for.

So that's briefly how Jamie came into our lives. It didn't, of course, happen overnight, there was the inevitable process; the background checks, the myriad interviews, the training courses, I'm sure you get the picture. But then Jamie arrived, fifteen years old, full of brooding attitude and anger at the world and not knowing what to do with it all. He was a tall gangly youth, his limbs long and skinny, appearing to jut out at awkward angles from his thin body and his shoulders were hunched as if he was trying to shrink to make himself inconspicuous. My first thoughts on seeing Jamie were of wanting to cook him a good meal, to put flesh on those bones, I also longed to greet him with a hug, but his body language shouted out that this would not be welcome. Jamie's social worker had been very honest with us before we agreed to take him, telling us that his mother had died of a drug overdose when he was four, and his father was an alcoholic, not the best role model for a boy. Jamie had been in and out of care all his life, and at the tender age of fifteen, it had been decided that he would never be able to return to his father, all previous attempts having failed miserably and he needed somewhere more permanent, with stability to prepare him for adult life. She painted such a bleak picture of Jamie that it was difficult to hold onto the fact that he was still a child, a damaged child yes, but he had the right to a better life and it was to be our role to provide it. Now you can see why this needed much thought and soul searching before we jumped in there. But jump in we did.

Jamie arrived to stay in the spring, entering our home with more of a swagger than a walk, eyebrows knitted into a scowl and lips curled purposefully down as if his demeanour was giving us some kind of message. Quiet and surly and answering questions with the briefest of nods, he'd seen it all before, we could tell and was determined not to be impressed. The social worker could hardly get out quick enough and I can't say that I blamed her. We had of course met Jamie before, several times, supervised visits with a 'minder' from social services, and eventually we'd been encouraged to take him out, unchaperoned. These had been rather quiet visits, quite unnatural really and we hoped things would be easier in our home situation.

I showed Jamie to his room. It had been Emma's bedroom and as yet we had done little to change it, hoping that giving Jamie some input into the decor and furnishings would, in some measure make him feel as if this was his room, his home. We explained that we had planned a trip to Ikea and told him what his budget would be for making this his own space. The only response was a shrug, the first of many!

During that first couple of weeks, I shed many tears over Jamie. He would respond to questions with a nod or a shrug, even though I tried to use 'open ended' questions as we had learned in training. He either genuinely didn't care about his life or decision making was so alien to him that he didn't know where to begin. I longed for him to understand that we were going to be there for him on a permanent basis, he'd been let down and had his hopes and expectations shattered so many times, it wasn't surprising that he didn't trust anyone.

I was becoming exhausted. My face ached with the effort of trying to appear bright and breezy. I had a constant headache and I was beginning to doubt the wisdom of embarking on this course. Pete, my husband was a brick. He too was struggling, but as I was the one who worked from home, (I'm a freelance illustrator), I seemed to bear the brunt of it. Yes, Jamie was out at school, (or so we hoped, he did have a history of truancy) but the hours spent at home were still uneasy for us all. We longed for him to feel that this was his home too. I ached when I watched his blank eyes and vacant expressions. It wasn't going to be easy, but we'd always known that and were in it for the long haul, there was no going back.

The Ikea trip was in some measure a success. We had drawn up a list of what was needed, leaving the colour and style choices for Jamie to make on the day. I love the quirky feel of Ikea, and had hoped that it was the kind of store which would appeal to a fifteen year old. Jamie showed very little interest at first, so we headed for the cafe and over a cup of tea narrowed the options down to what we felt was reasonable, and then handed the catalogue to Jamie to make the final decisions. It seemed to click then that he was the one who would have to live with this furniture, and at one point I thought a tiny smile quivered on his lips, but it could have been wishful thinking.
Returning home allowed me to escape to the kitchen and begin the evening meal whilst Pete tried to interest Jamie in assembling the flat packed furniture for his room, no easy task.

And so, the newest member of our family had a trendy new room with plenty of storage, a small desk and, as a welcome present, we bought Jamie his own laptop. In practical ways there was little more we could do, our plan was to remain constant in our day to day living, making allowances for Jamie to some degree, but giving clear boundaries in the hope that he would begin to feel secure in our care.

It was difficult to assess how happy Jamie felt, or indeed any other emotions he may have been experiencing. Communication was still only the bare minimum, but was this just the normal morose, scowling teenager, (a species we had lived with before), or was it Jamie's background which made him this way? It was impossible to tell.

Emma came to visit with regularity, joking that it was her baby son, Josh, who was the star attraction and I had to admit that to some extent she was right. Pete and I were still in raptures over this little boy whose very presence brought such happiness, even if he mostly snored through his time with us. One Saturday, when Emma came with Josh, we had what I now think of as our first breakthrough with Jamie. When our visitors arrived and the kettle was dutifully put on, I went upstairs, knocked on Jamie's bedroom door and popped my head in to tell him I was making coffee if he wanted to join us. I wasn't sure if the response meant yes or no, but the offer was there so I crossed my fingers and hoped he'd come down. When he didn't, Emma offered to take the coffee to his room. Josh was upstairs asleep in his travel cot and she wanted to check on him. Emma was good with Jamie, displaying a natural easy going attitude which I hoped could reach where we couldn't, but she was downstairs again in only a couple of minutes.

"He said thanks for the coffee and Josh is still sound asleep. I've asked Jamie to let us know if he wakes and we don't hear him." The cunning Emma had a plan.

"Was that the baby?" Peter asked a few minutes later.
"No." Emma was emphatic.
"I think it was love." I joined in, "Shall I go and get him?"
"No." Our daughter insisted.
Two minutes later, Jamie appeared in the doorway, holding our grandson. My heart leapt into my throat. Jamie was smiling and holding Josh with such tenderness, I could have cried. Emma didn't bat an eyelid.
"Oh, he's awake, I didn't hear him." Our daughter lied blatantly!
"S'okay." Jamie replied. "D'you think he'd like to come into the garden with me?"
"Good idea Jamie, but put his little jacket on first will you?" Emma passed the jacket to Jamie and he sat down with Josh on his knee to put it on. The two then vanished into the garden. I was speechless, well for all of ten seconds anyway.
"Will he be alright?" I asked my daughter.
"Which one?" she smiled.
We could see the garden from the window and watched in amazement as Jamie walked up and down, jogging a chuckling Josh in his arms. Was this our sullen, moody foster son? It was a small thing, but it gave me such hope to see Jamie smiling and taking an interest in the baby. Maybe he felt some sort of bond with him, I don't know. Whatever it was I was so moved by the sight and so filled with hope that I struggled to fight back the tears bubbling up inside of me.

Jamie brought Josh back inside after about ten minutes, but the spell wasn't quite broken.
"I think he's hungry." Jamie told Emma.
"Would you keep him a few minutes while I warm his bottle?" she asked.

Jamie nodded and grinned. I was amazed; I didn't think I'd ever seen him smile like that. What was even better, when Emma came back with the bottle, Jamie asked if he could give it to him. With very little prompting from Emma, Jamie successfully managed to get him to take all his feed, with a couple of respectable burps in the bargain. This was proving to be a remarkable breakthrough.

Of course the visit had to end and Jamie once again returned to his room leaving us to ponder what had happened. Yes it was a positive step forward but Jamie's problems couldn't be solved by one little triumph. The days to come were to bring more difficulties.

I had long suspected that Jamie was taking money from my purse. Pete and I had decided to ignore the first couple of times, but when it continued we knew we had to confront him. Calling Jamie down from his room we told him that we needed to talk. The body language was immediately hostile and I had a sudden urge to run to the telephone and ring for Emma to bring the baby round again.
"Jamie, money has been taken from Sarah's purse and we need to get it sorted out." Pete began. The atmosphere could be cut with the proverbial knife.
"In a household of just three people, it's pretty obvious who is taking it." He continued, "Is there a reason you need extra money? If your pocket money isn't enough we can talk about it."
Jamie was silent, scowling down at the table as if that was the culprit. Then suddenly he shocked us both.
"D'you want me to leave then?" he asked, in such a matter of fact tone that suggested he felt this was the natural progression in our relationship.

"No, certainly not!" I jumped in, "We only want to know why you took it; this is your home Jamie, for as long as you want."

Another shrug, but I could see the confusion in his eyes. Was he testing us perhaps? It was difficult to tell. Pete suggested that we left the matter alone, telling Jamie that if he needed extra money, the best way to go about it was by talking and we would try to sort something out. Jamie was obviously perplexed by this, seeming to have expected a huge row leading to his going back into the care of social services. I couldn't imagine how that must feel; living in fear of being rejected and sent back into the 'system'. It's no wonder he was confused and insecure.

The bond with our grandson and Jamie had got us thinking about getting a pet. Emma couldn't keep running round with Josh in an effort to provide some kind of therapy for Jamie, so, being animal lovers ourselves, we broached the subject of a dog.

"Would it be my dog, or yours?" Jamie was certainly interested.

"If you think you could look after one I don't see why it couldn't be yours if that's what you'd like?" Pete replied.

"So, if I move on, like, would I take it with me?"

That remark cut deep. He was obviously still insecure.

"Jamie, we really don't want you to move on. We'd like you to think of us as parents, or at least family. We want you to stay." I looked hopefully at him. "And we hope that's what you want too." I added.

Jamie made a sudden leap from the chair he was sitting on and ran off upstairs as if being pursued by a demon. Pete and I were left staring at each other, wondering what we had said to bring such a response. Tentatively I followed Jamie to his room and knocked on the door. No answer. I tried again with the same effect and this time opened the door, quietly calling his name. Jamie was laid prostrate on his bed his thin body wracked with huge sobs. For a moment I couldn't breathe, it was one of those seconds that takes forever to pass. Pete was close behind me and gently pushed me inside whispering that he'd be there if I needed him. I no longer resisted the impulse to hug Jamie. He may have been fifteen years old and as tall as me, but I needed him to know how wanted he really was. It suddenly hit me that when he mentioned leaving, I was frightened of it actually happening. I sat on the edge of the bed and pulled him towards me. To my surprise, he didn't resist. With his bony arms reaching around my neck, he sobbed openly onto my shoulder. We stayed like that for possibly a decade, I don't know, but I was crying too and, I suspect, so was Pete.

I can't say that this incident made everything perfect from that time, but it was certainly a defining moment and our relationship from then on began to gel. We went the next day to the animal sanctuary and Jamie chose a black and white mongrel dog who wooed him with big soft brown eyes and a lolling tongue with which he gave us all the once over. There is definitely a bond between the boy and the dog and we all get so much pleasure from them both. Jamie has been with us for nearly two years now. He's doing well at school, studying for 'A' levels, and at home, (which it really is for him now), well we still have our ups and downs, but hey, who doesn't? As it is with families this story does not have an ending. Each day is a new beginning and we thank God for bringing Jamie into our lives, not only for what we could give him but for what he has given, and continues to give, to us.

The End

With Love…

Dear Aunt Geraldine,
Thank you so much for the lovely embroidered tray cloth which arrived this morning. I shall put it away with the antimacassars you sent for my birthday. Yes, it is difficult to buy such items these days and I really do appreciate the effort you put into finding them for me. I haven't literally got a 'bottom drawer' as you suggested, but I'm keeping them in a rather pretty sea grass basket, lined with floral cotton. I am sure they'll come in useful one day.

In answer to your question, no, I haven't found Mr. Right yet, but honestly I'm in no hurry. Yes I know it's nearly three years since Simon died and I love you for all the support you've given me since that awful day. Maybe I wasn't destined to be a bride, but I don't really think I'm in danger of becoming an old maid Aunt G. Things are different these days, careers are important to women and I love my job at the animal sanctuary: I get all the affection and sloppy kisses I could want there.

Mum sends her love. She says its ages since you came to stay and you know you're always welcome. We were pleased to hear you'd taken on a lodger cum companion, Chrissie isn't it? Mums delighted she's a medical student; she seems to think that speaks volumes about her character and it's great that she helps with the garden and can drive you about a bit too.

Must go now, I'm on late shift at work, got to see a man about a dog, ha ha!
With love, Lizzie xx

Dear Aunt Geraldine,
What a great idea to protect my linens with mothballs. Actually I have some sweet little sachets of lavender that I might use instead but thanks for the tip.

Please don't worry about my job; I am very careful about letting the dogs lick my face. You really shouldn't keep sending me presents but you are right, it can be cold exercising the dogs and the thermal vests will be useful. I know I'm your favourite great-niece, but could that be because I'm your only one?

It sounds as if you and Chrissie had a great day up in London. She is brave to drive into the city; I'd take the tube any day. Mum thinks she sounds like the ideal lodger, but she's a little concerned about the peppercorn rent arrangement. I'm to tell you she'll ring soon.

It is only a couple of weeks since you last asked, but no, I haven't found a beau yet. It isn't a case of not trying Aunt G; I really do have a full and interesting social life. As for the Internet dating you warned me about, don't worry, I have no intention of doing anything so outrageous. It's not really a matter of finding someone who will match up to Simon. You know I was devastated after the accident and no one could ever replace him, but if someone comes along then fine, I'm just not in any hurry.

Have you decided when you're coming to visit? I'm due a couple of day's holiday so I could spend some time with you. Let us know, bye for now,

With love, Lizzie x x

Dear Aunt Geraldine

I'm so glad you're enjoying knitting again and the tea cosy is lovely, thank you. Those tiny little egg cosies match beautifully; they must have taken you ages to make.

We're so pleased you can come and stay and of course Chrissie can come too, there's bags of room and it will be good to meet her. I must admit to a little jealousy. Your description and all she does makes me feel quite inferior, but I'm sure we'll get along if you like her and it will be much better being chauffeured rather than struggling with your bags on the train. I've taken three days off work to

make a long weekend, so I thought a trip to the coast would be fun one day with a posh picnic perhaps? We'll see how you feel when you arrive. Looking forward to seeing you.
With love, Lizzie x x

Dear Aunt Geraldine,
What was it you used to call me when I was a mischievous child, a scallywag wasn't it? Well I think that term applies to you now! If I didn't love you so much I may not be so polite and tell you that you're a crafty conniving old witch! You deliberately let me think "Chrissie" was a girl! Okay, I know you have a habit of adding 'ie' to everyone's name, it certainly stuck with me, but I think you planned this from the beginning. It could have been embarrassing if I had made up the spare bed in my room for Chris as I intended, thank heavens Mum decided to spring clean the attic and put him in there instead.

I could tell how much you two thought of each other as soon as I saw the hand knitted socks he was wearing. As for your funny turn on the morning we were due to go to the coast, well that was just blatant. What's worse is that I'm pretty sure you'd roped Mum into the conspiracy by then. Even Chris could see through that one. I was so embarrassed: what should have been a day out for the four of us turning into almost a date. You didn't really need Mum to stay behind to look after you did you?

Of course I'll have to forgive you. You didn't actually tell any lies about Chris; he is very attractive and intelligent, with a great personality. He apparently loves dogs as well as little old ladies. And I can't argue that we're unsuited, we got on really well on our day out together, and it was good of him to take me for a meal the following day to say thank you.

Aunt G, you are terrible really; a matchmaker, an old fashioned romantic, but I must admit you have excellent taste. Between you and me, I do rather like Chris and it's the first time I've felt like this since Simon. He tells me that you want him to bring you up for a few days next month as well. Can I count on one of your funny turns again? Bless you Aunt G; you always did know what was best for me, even before I did. To be honest with you, I've been working so hard lately that I feel I could do with a little break myself. Could I come and stay with you next weekend?

Looking forward to hearing from you and thanks for all the lovely presents,

With love, Lizzie x x

The End

Waiting
The lady's attire would have been more in keeping in a seedy nightclub.

The catering industry hadn't served success on a plate to Frank. He had worked hard to achieve his coveted position, starting his career in hot, steamy kitchens, washing up and preparing vegetables. He'd suffered temperamental chefs in respectful silence, taking blame when it was mis-placed and grovelling at times to keep his job. He had studied hard and learned from every position he'd ever held.

Moving into serving in the restaurants was his aim, starting as a lowly waiter and using the experience gained from handling pretentious chefs into placating grumbling customers. Frank's efforts were eventually rewarded and he found his dream job as Maître d at an exclusive country hotel. Frank loved the work, long hours were a pleasure and he took pride in every aspect of the job.

The owner was content to leave the smooth running of the restaurant to Frank, and rarely put in an appearance, preferring to stay in his luxury suite-cum-office, with meals served to him in privacy. This suited all the hotel staff and any problem which needed his attention was a rare occasion indeed.

And so it happened that one day, Frank welcomed a young couple into his exclusive domain and knew instinctively that trouble lay in waiting. As the pair entered the restaurant, Frank raised his eyebrows. They couldn't have been any closer together if they had been Siamese twins, with their arms contorted around each other and her head on his shoulder. The lady's attire in itself would have been more in keeping with a seedy night-club rather than an exclusive hotel dining room, what little of it there was that is. Other diners turned to stare. Some smiled but most looked disapprovingly at the young couple, who were oblivious to all but each other. Frank bristled, his was a high class restaurant; there was a certain decorum expected from patrons.

Unfortunately the table reserved for the pair, table eight, was in full view of the room and being fully booked that evening, Frank had no choice but to seat them there. Within minutes the waiter was in for another shock, the young lady had removed her shoes and they began playing 'footsie' beneath the table, with no regard whatsoever for other diners! Frank marched over and coughed to gain their attention.
"Would you care to see the wine menu sir?" he asked in an effort to remind them they were in a public place.
The couple didn't look away from each other's eyes.
"Yes, thank you" was the curt reply.
"And some water?" Frank would not be deterred.
"Fine... whatever." The young man waved dismissively at him, and they resumed stroking each other's hands as well as feet. Frank was aghast and aware that other guests were watching. He moved away to fetch a jug of water, feeling the colour rising from his neck to his face. Dropping the ice cubes into the jug, Frank could hear the young woman squealing in a high pitched voice which irritated to his very core. He shuddered and returned to the table with the iced water, hoping it would cool their ardour.

"May I recommend the lobster platter this evening?" Frank had true staying power.
"Ugh, not seafood!" the young woman shrieked in a voice that resounded like a bell throughout the room. Her partner laughed loudly, still not meeting the waiter's stare.

"Try some darling, you may surprise yourself," her companion encouraged. But 'darling' continued to giggle and shriek, quite inappropriately, Frank thought as he hovered to take their order. The young man was becoming annoyed at the waiter's continued presence at his elbow, finally taking his eyes off the lady and looking directly at Frank.
"How about a little privacy while we decide?" he snapped, his flashing eyes reflecting his irritation.

Frank moved away piqued and busied himself with a more appreciative client, still very aware of the noise from the table eight. After a reasonable interval, he returned to the couple to take their order, trying his best to be polite when he would gladly have thrown them out of his restaurant. The couple ordered their food and a rather good bottle of wine to go with it. Frank couldn't fault the young man's taste, except perhaps in women.
The order was dispatched to the kitchen and the waiter uncorked the wine and returned to table eight for the gentleman to taste.

It was then that it happened, the details were a little hazy to Frank afterwards, he couldn't understand how it had occurred and it was certainly a first in his entire career. One moment he was pouring the wine, watching the ruby red liquid swirl in the glass, and the next minute he had knocked the lady's glass from the table and a trickle of red was running down the front of her dress. Naturally, it being delicate cream wool, the dress absorbed the wine thirstily, flowing downwards to puddle in her lap. For a split second, myriad thoughts ran through Frank's mind. Had he really done that? Surely he had only fantasized about such an act; was this a Freudian moment and his sub-conscious had taken over? The whole room seemed to be in an uproar, as the woman screamed and fussed, dabbing at her dress, which only served to enlarge the stain. The young man jumped up and pulled Frank towards him by his lapels. Frank braced himself thinking he was going to be punched, but the blow wasn't physical. "You did that on purpose!" shouted the man. Frank shook his head, dumbstruck, no longer in control of his domain.

"Fetch the owner!" Shouted the angry young man, "and tell him his son would like to see him!"

The End

The Bridge
Gwen couldn't remember life before Jack.

Gwen sat on the warped, weathered bench, as she had so often done in the past, giving her aching feet a rest whilst gazing fondly at the old bridge. Although small, it was a beautiful structure, stone built with the usual signs of age, moss and lichen appearing to hold the stones together. The view from the bench was charming, what Gwen would have called a 'chocolate box picture' although chocolates were packaged differently these days. The boxes displayed on shelves in the village store when she was a young girl depicted scenes of thatched roofed cottages or a basket of kittens. They were very often chosen for the picture alone rather than the contents. Gwen still had one of those boxes in her wardrobe, stuffed full of all the letters Jack had written to her during the war years. Dear Jack, he hadn't been much of a one for writing, yet he'd faithfully sent those letters, although short and with almost as much struck out by the censors as he had managed to write.

Gwen couldn't remember life before Jack. They had grown up together in this same village, living only four doors apart in the terrace of houses facing the village green. Jack's parents ran the grocery store and her Dad worked as a labourer at one of the surrounding farms. Born within a few days of each other, they were inseparable as children, playing in each other's back parlour, or cricket on the green if the weather allowed. For a girl, Jack had to admit, she had considerable potential as a spin bowler. They had both attended the village school, a one-class affair with a happy family atmosphere. Gwen thought about the seemingly endless summer holidays when the days were long and the sun was hot. She and Jack had played by this bridge. From on top they could see their homes on one side and the church, where they would later be married, on the other. They had thrown sticks from the bridge, or raced paper boats when the stream was swollen from the spring rains. When it was hot they took off their socks and shoes, dangling their feet in the cool water, or paddled with their fishing nets and jam jars, catching tiddlers. Jack was like a brother to Gwen, perhaps even closer than her own two brothers with whom she squabbled constantly. It wasn't until they were both fourteen that she thought of Jack as something more than a brother. As they were standing on the bridge, watching a family of moorhens drifting by with the current, Jack shyly kissed her on the cheek. Gwen was startled but turned to smile at him, returning the kiss with a gentle peck on his lips. From that moment their relationship changed. They were still as close and saw each other as frequently as before, but whenever they were together, they held hands and when they parted company, a brief kiss became their routine. Gwen knew, even then, that there would never be anyone but Jack for her.

The change in their relationship came at the same time as the outbreak of the Second World War. Both their fathers went off to fight and village life was no longer the uncomplicated endless summer it had always seemed to be. The whole community was stunned when Jack's father became one of the first casualties of war. Jack grew up very quickly after that, longing for the day he would be old enough to take his father's place at the battlefront, a day Gwen hoped and prayed would never come, but inevitably it did.

Sighing as she watched the leaves beginning to fall from the trees in the churchyard, Gwen made a conscious effort to divert her thoughts from those dark days, remembering instead the elation that the end of the war brought. Her Jack came home safely, the same, but different, and they began getting to know each other all over again, putting the war behind them and looking to the future. Their wedding was one of the first to be held in the village church at the end of the war. Friends and neighbours rallied round to make it an extra special occasion, celebrating not only Gwen and Jack's marriage, but also the beginning of a new and better future for them all. As many newlywed couples did in those days, Gwen moved in with her new husband and his widowed mother, helping out in the store to ease the older woman's burden and Jack found work in engineering at a factory in the nearby town.

Gwen shuffled her stiff legs to a more comfortable position on the hard bench, smiling as she recalled those early days of marriage. The children came along almost straight away, a girl first, and then twin boys. Jack was so proud and worked long hours to provide for them and when at home, he couldn't do enough to make their childhood as idyllic as his and Gwen's had been. As the children grew up they left the village in search of work. Living in the country was no longer the same for the young people or for Gwen and Jack. The village store inevitably closed down as people shopped in the new supermarkets on the outskirts of town. The village school also closed, no longer viable with fewer children in the village than ever before. Gwen reluctantly watched her own family become independent and move away, but she still had her Jack and they were as close as ever, sweethearts and best friends.

Of course, now there were the grandchildren, seven of them, and they were all but grown up and independent too. Gwen shivered, pulling the collar up on her coat, it was getting cooler and she'd have to be going soon. Her thoughts moved on quickly, recalling those earlier years with such clarity, and inevitably at this particular time, many of the memories brought a tear to her eye. But Gwen had always been one to count her blessings and she reckoned she'd had more than her fair share throughout the years. So what if she didn't see as much of her family as she would have liked, they were good to her and kept in touch, besides she would see them all tomorrow. They were coming from all parts of the country, not only her children and grandchildren but her brothers too. The little Church would be full again as it was for her wedding day, only the faces would be different, so many loved ones missing as life had marched on.

Suddenly Gwen stood up. She would walk over the bridge again before returning home. It held so many memories and had been the scene of many significant events throughout her life. Looking down at the slow moving water, Gwen wondered how she would cope with tomorrow. With so many friends and family coming she had worried about providing accommodation and a meal for them all, but her daughter had taken it out of her hands for which Gwen was truly grateful. Since turning eighty she was no longer able to cater for more than a handful of visitors and was content to let Susan take over. Her daughter was a capable, organized woman who took these things in her stride and of course she had daughters of her own to help.

Gwen was so engrossed in thought that at first she didn't notice that she was no longer alone on the bridge. Watching the water meander under the bridge, she became aware of the warmth of another person beside her. She turned smiling, and looked into the face of her beloved Jack who took her hand in both of his and gently kissed her soft cheek.

"Here you are." he said, "I was beginning to think you'd changed your mind, or run off with another feller!"
Gwen laughed, "Reckon it's a bit late for that now. The church is booked and I'm more than happy to renew my vows if you are?"
Jack squeezed her hand as they turned to go home. "I've never wanted anything else but you my love." Smiling at his wife of sixty years, hand in hand they walked as one, over the bridge and back to their cottage on the green, their conversation turning to the future and the next day's celebration of their diamond-wedding anniversary.

The End

A Good Day's Work

*A deliciously wicked plan was taking root
in Glenys' mind*

Glenys put the novel down, slightly disappointed that once again she had guessed the ending. "Maybe I should try writing murder mysteries." Glenys spoke aloud to no-one in particular.

"Did you say something love?" Roger asked, hardly opening his eyes.

"No. Go back to sleep, it's not dinner time yet!" Studying her husband of twenty years it was difficult to recall whatever it was she had seen in him, a self-obsessed hypochondriac, whose only real illness was an allergy to work. He had sleep disorders, blood disorders, nervous trouble, bowel trouble and goodness knows what else. Roger even reckoned he'd had swine flu twice! Yes, he really enjoyed ill-health.

Glenys placed the book back on the shelf with the hundred or so others she had read and went to start the dinner. Reading was an escape. Life with Roger was dull and uneventful to say the least and loosing herself in the plot of a good book was the only excitement that life offered these days. Mulling over the latest story line, Glenys thought that perhaps it wasn't writing which could change her life, but murder. Hadn't she read enough books to commit the perfect crime? She knew an alibi was crucial to the success of any crime; arranging one was child's play. The weapon and opportunity would take a little more thought, which was certainly not impossible to Glenys's fertile imagination. And what motive could anyone suspect? To family and friends they were a devoted couple, living a happy but quiet life due to

Roger's failing health. A deliciously wicked plan was taking root in Glenys's mind.

Never one to waste time, Glenys began preparations the minute Roger went upstairs to bed. She wouldn't rush, tomorrow would be soon enough! Tonight all that needed to be done was to sharpen the wire and make a phone call.

Jen was delighted to accept her friends offer to meet for lunch the next day and as Glenys had expected, she insisted on using her car, picking her up sharp at ten o'clock. Jen could always be relied upon to be punctual.

Glenys made sure Roger had a bad night, keeping the telly on loud, and making several trips to the loo, flushing as noisily as possible. She thoughtfully kept popping her head round the bedroom door to enquire if Roger was sleeping well. When Glenys herself retired, she unfortunately made a mistake setting the alarm, causing it to ring loudly for several minutes. Roger was livid; didn't she know he needed his sleep? Glenys apologized profusely and offered to make some cocoa. She also suggested that perhaps another of those little pills from the doctor would help him sleep. Roger downed another pill and turned over. Glenys climbed in beside him and waited until he snored. If she woke him once, she woke him a dozen times. For her, adrenaline was a natural stimulant, keeping her awake and excited about tomorrow.

At eight o'clock, Glenys let the alarm clock ring until she was certain Roger was wide awake. He grumbled loudly and his wife sympathised, suggesting a morning in bed to help recover from his bad night. Perhaps another of those sleeping pills would soothe his nerves? Glenys brought him a nice cup of tea, (laced with another three little pills), and one for him to take. Roger read the morning paper until he began to feel sleepy.

There was less than an hour to set the scene. When the snoring began, (a noise that would certainly not be missed) she set to work. Firstly to stage the break in. No problem. She broke the glass panel in the kitchen door, leading into the conservatory, (the conservatory door was always left ajar for the cat), and naturally did this from the outside. Then she pulled out several drawers, scattering the contents randomly about the room. Upstairs, while Roger snored on, she rifled her jewellery box, dropping a few trinkets into her handbag.

Nine forty-five, it was time! Glenys took the wire she'd sharpened the night before and stood over her sleeping husband. Spittle was drooling from his mouth as he slept the sleep of the dead, (well, soon anyway!) Glenys pulled back the duvet and began probing her husband's chest. Finding the exact spot she carefully inserted the wire. Roger startled and tried to open his heavy eyes.

"It's all right dear, just a bad dream." Her voice was soothing, almost loving. His eyes closed again, so deeply asleep that he hardly felt the wire moving into his chest.

Jen was reliably prompt. A chirpy Glenys shouted goodbye to Roger, then jumped into the car with her friend. A shopping trip and lunch out was the kind of treat she felt she deserved.

Three hours later, Glenys invited Jen into the house for a coffee. They knew all was not well when they saw the mess in the lounge.

"Roger!" Glenys screamed running upstairs, followed closely by Jen. Roger looked quite peaceful really, although a little pale. Glenys sobbed and cried over his body until Jen pulled her away and steered her downstairs.

The police were remarkably quick and very understanding. Glenys explained how Roger had slept badly and insisted on an extra couple of sleeping pills, against her better judgement of course. The doctor prescribed a sedative and she attempted to answer the policeman's questions even though she was so obviously distraught. Yes, Roger was on medication to thin his blood, perhaps that's why he seemed to bleed so profusely from such a small wound. No, she could think of nothing small and sharp which could have been used as a weapon.

Eventually the circus was over and everyone left. Roger had been taken to the morgue and Glenys insisted she would be fine on her own. She was delighted with how the plan had worked out. The murder weapon was the puzzle. Glenys knew how hard it was to solve a murder without the weapon. A glass of sherry might be more appropriate than a cup of tea she thought, settling down to begin another murder mystery. But first, Glenys took out her sewing kit, removed a sharpened curve of wire from her handbag and began to sew it back under the cup of her bra.

The End

Coming of Age

Miriam was stunned. For the first time she began to see things from Chloe's perspective.

The sampler had been an impulse buy. They had always held a fascination for Miriam as she imagined the stories they could tell of the young girls who put so much time and effort into making them. This particular one was dated 1867, with the name *'Susannah Golding, Age Twelve'* neatly sewn into the pattern. Although well over a hundred years old the colours were still vibrant. Studying the needlepoint symbols of nature; birds, flowers, a sturdy tree and a border of sycamore leaves; they spoke of youth and life and hope for the future. Miriam could almost see the twelve year old girl working the intricate design by candlelight, striving to become accomplished in the skills which would make her a good wife. She wondered what Susannah's hopes and dreams had been, her aspirations?

Inevitably Miriam's thoughts turned to her granddaughter. Chloe had been twelve when the accident had occurred, shattering their perfect family life and so cruelly snatching away Chloe's future. An athletic girl, full of life and laughter, in the wrong place at the wrong time. The lorry driver had lost control, they would probably never know why and Chloe's life shifted to another course from that moment on.

"Lucky to be alive" the doctors said, but Miriam could see nothing lucky about the situation at all. Months in hospital followed by rehabilitation returned a very different Chloe to her family. Still their beautiful girl, a teenager by then, but she would never walk again.

Chloe had changed, grown up too soon with challenges and cares a child should never have to face. And her family had changed too. Their lifestyle needed to alter to accommodate Chloe's chair. Yes there was a measure of support and financial help, but it could never take away the stark reality of what had happened. Miriam feared for her granddaughter's future; when she and Chloe's parents were gone, who would look after her? And now today they were to celebrate her eighteenth birthday. Miriam carefully wrapped the sampler, hoping Chloe would like it as much as she did.

Walking through her daughter's house and into the garden, Miriam paused to watch the family gathered around Chloe and listened to their laughter, feeling a pride and warmth flooding through her body. The group opened immediately to include her, and she picked up the end of a conversation about Chloe's acceptance at university.

"It's got the best political science department in the country." She was telling them. "The library's fantastic and the halls of residence are something else!"

"I thought it was the bars which were the priority for new students!" Her brother David teased, making Chloe laugh.

Miriam knew her granddaughter had plans for university, but feared it would be too much for the girl to cope with. It was one thing to have a degree of independence among family and friends but would she feel isolated away from home? Chloe didn't seem to understand how vulnerable she was.

The barbeque was sizzling and the party proceeded with music, food and wine occupying everyone's attention. Chloe looked radiant. Miriam had to admit she was a plucky girl and had continued attending the same school after the accident, quickly catching up on the work missed during her recovery. Previous energy and love of sports seemed to be channelled into more academic subjects as Chloe joined the debating society and took an interest in the law and politics. Excellent 'A' level results justified the hard work and long hours Chloe had studied and Miriam was so proud of her granddaughter, but so fearful for her future.

"Hi Grandma!" Chloe broke into her daydream. "Is that parcel for me or are you holding onto it for posterity!"

"Sorry darling, I was miles away. Of course it's for you, here."

Chloe grinned and began tearing at the paper, looking like a little girl again. Carefully lifting the sampler, her eyes sparkled.

"Oh Gran, its lovely!"

"Do you like it? I hoped you would." Chloe traced her fingers over the glass, outlining the delicate stitching.

"It's beautiful! Just think of all the hours that must have been spent working on it. 'Susannah Golding', I'll have to do a bit of research to see what I can find out about her. She must have been born when, 1855?"

Miriam was thrilled that Chloe seemed to genuinely like the sampler, knowing that most of the family would think it a strange gift, but seeing her granddaughter's face validated the choice.

"Look at the colours and oh, those swallows and a nest in the tree! Thanks Gran, it's perfect."

As grandmother and granddaughter sat alone in a corner of the garden the girl seemed to sense what Miriam was feeling.

"You know, I'm going to be fine at uni Gran. I've been longing for this for years. Mum and Dad have been great, as have you and David, but I'm not a little girl anymore. I know you all mean well, but you can't keep me wrapped in cotton wool forever. I need to spread my wings, or should I say 'roll my wheels!' I love you all and I'll always be grateful for how you've cared for me, but I have to move on. There are fantastic facilities for wheelchair users at uni, and I can't wait to make new friends."

Miriam was stunned. For the first time she began to see things from Chloe's perspective. Could they have been smothering her? It hadn't occurred to her before. Chloe was gazing at the sampler as she changed the subject.

"I wonder what Susannah Golding's life was like? No chance of university for her. Accomplished in needlepoint, piano playing and schooled in etiquette I suppose, to make someone a good wife. How terrible, what a waste of a life, but she didn't have today's options did she? Shall I tell you a secret Gran?"

Miriam nodded, enthralled by Chloe's little speech.

"I have political ambitions!" She grinned at the startled look on her grandmother's face.

"Well, why not? I may be only eighteen, but I know how to work hard. And if Franklin D. Roosevelt can govern America from a wheelchair, why can't I be prime minister one day!" Chloe laughed at Miriam's open mouth.

"Shall we get back to the party?" she smiled.

In all of her sixty six years Miriam felt she had never received such a sound, although unintentional, reproach. She had looked upon her granddaughter with pity, when the girl deserved nothing but admiration for such a brave outlook on life. She had certainly learned a lesson that day, one which gave her a new insight into Chloe's character. Miriam happily followed her granddaughter back to the others to celebrate the coming of age of a truly inspiring young woman.

The End

Always the Bridesmaid.

"Make sure you catch the bouquet..."

My mother's jaw dropped in horror! "But Jayne, this will be the third time you've been a bridesmaid and you know what they say, never the bride and all that!" Mum means well but you can't turn down attending your best friend at her wedding just because of some ancient superstition, can you? Anyway, I don't subscribe to such ideas, touch wood.

"Make sure you catch the bouquet..." Mum went on and on.

"Mum! That's so old fashioned, and what makes you think I want to be the next one to be married? Twenty eight's hardly on the shelf, is it?" I challenged her, only to receive one of those knowing looks and a wry smile. I knew when to concede to my mother's wisdom and quickly changed the subject.

The wedding merry-go-round had begun with a vengeance and I found myself being dragged round every bridal shop in the city. But Rachel's enthusiasm was infectious and I had to admit that I enjoyed our first few shopping trips, until about the fifth consecutive weekend. Yes, I was delighted for my friend, she and Gareth were so obviously made for each other, but I had other things to do during my precious weekend hours... well, I had been promising myself I'd re-grout the bathroom tiles for ages, and my library books were well overdue! Rachel had to understand that I had a life of my own. Each time she tried on a wedding dress she preened and sighed in front of the mirror,

"Do you think Gareth will like me in this one?" she enquired for the twenty something time. Perhaps here I should confess to feeling just a teeny bit jealous of my best friend. Rachel is as near perfect a specimen as anyone could wish to be; a consummate size ten, with obedient tresses of naturally blonde hair which framed her exquisite heart shaped face and set off striking blue eyes. She would have looked incredible wearing a sack. What made me even more covetous was that her personality was every bit as beautiful as she was. Everyone loved her and deservedly so, she was the full package.

This being my third time as a bridesmaid, I was becoming something of an expert. The hen night was child's play. No, literally, it was. With my considerable experience of organising such events, I had encountered many of the pitfalls that can happen when giggling girls and alcohol are mixed in large quantities. Rachel wasn't into that kind of night out and begged me to stick to innocent fun with nothing embarrassing, so in my wisdom, I hired a rather large bouncy castle and then struggled to find an indoor venue to accommodate it. The local community centre eventually fitted the bill and we were all set, a couple of hours behaving like children, then a quiet meal at Rachel's favourite Indian, simple, innocent fun. What could possibly go wrong?

The A&E department of the general hospital was extremely busy that Saturday night. Obviously if I had known that the bride-to-be was going to break her leg slipping off the bouncy castle, I would have chosen a quieter night. There were also as many alcohol fumes in the waiting area as there would have been had we settled on a night out clubbing but Rachel was extremely gracious about it all and lay patiently on the hospital trolley, trying hard not to wince with pain. I think perhaps I was suffering more than she was. I certainly felt guilty knowing that her dream of walking down the aisle would never happen; a wheelchair takes some of the romance out of a wedding. Then I would have to face her parents, they had trusted me to look after Rachel and I had assured them that I would, and Gareth too. What he was going to say was best not to think about.

At least there was a week to become accustomed to the plaster cast before the wedding. The father of the bride would just have to push his daughter down the aisle and for some of the photographs we planned to prop Rachel up or at least disguise the chair with the voluminous fabric of the dress, sensitive angles and posing; the photographer seemed to relish the challenge. Gareth took care of the necessary changes to the honeymoon plans and the hotel happily changed their room to a ground floor suite.

On the plus side, Rachel had an unexpected full week off work before the wedding, which she actually needed to adjust to her newly limited mobility. I of course tried my best to be useful, and not only from a sense of guilt. I really wanted my friend to enjoy her day. On the Monday evening before the wedding, I arrived at Rachel's house to help her decide the final seating plan for the reception, always a tricky business. She was playing around with place cards when I arrived and seemed to have most of the plan complete.
"There are just a few problems to iron out," she told me, "Mainly where to seat Uncle Harry."
"Why?" I asked, "Is he difficult to get on with, halitosis, b.o. or two heads?"
"Oh no, nothing like that," Rachel chuckled, "It's just that he's so painfully shy, we need to sit him with someone who'll bring him out of his shell. He's never married and has no one to bring to the wedding. Perhaps

I'll just put him with Aunt Gladys's family, they're a lively bunch!"

We soon had the seating plan all sorted out and I was all for opening a celebratory bottle of plonk when Rachel went all serious on me.

"Jayne, could I ask a big favour of you?"

She had me there didn't she? How could I refuse anything while I still felt terrible about the hen party?

"After the reception could you look after Uncle Harry for me? He's such a dear and he's on his own and... well you know, he's so shy and everything, and you don't have a partner for the evening reception do you? I wouldn't ask, but he is my favourite uncle and I haven't seen him for ages. I need to know someone's looking out for him."

Great, I thought, just what I need, to be lumbered with a shy morose uncle! But of course, I smiled and agreed happily, just hoping he wasn't the sort to get drunk and maudlin at family weddings.

All things considered, the week went pretty smoothly and eventually the big day arrived. I stayed overnight at Rachel's house then we began the big day with a trip to the hairdressers. A little pampering was just the thing to steady the nerves and we returned coiffed and manicured to perfection. Well, Rachel looked perfect even with the plaster cast. I, as usual, felt like plain Jayne in comparison, but I managed to stifle my own feelings to concentrate on the bride.

The sun shone, the service was meaningful and enough tears were shed to comply with tradition. Gareth looked extremely handsome in his tuxedo and Rachel, as ever, was stunning. The photographer did a really good job with the photos, positioning the happy couple in some quite romantic poses, you know the sort, he looking lovingly down as she gazed up into his eyes. It almost reduced me to tears. And the reception certainly lived up to expectations. It was a fantastic country hotel, oozing with charm and character. Tea and sarnies would have been romantic in that setting, but the meal was out of this world. Three courses of pure ambrosia. I had to restrain myself from finishing off the bride's untouched meal. (Could that be why she is so thin and I'm so...well, curvy?)

I was slightly distracted during the meal by table three, where Aunt Gladys and her family sat with Uncle Harry. I recognised Gladys from some photos at Rachel's house and also because she is the image of Rachel's mum. Her family were all grown up and although I couldn't remember their names, it didn't matter, all I was interested in was Uncle Harry, I needed to know what to expect. As I looked around the table, I could identify Gladys's two daughters, a giggly pair dressed in overkill, and her son, looking slightly embarrassed at his sisters' behaviour. Uncle Harry sat opposite Gladys, slurping up his raspberry pavlova and cream as if he had been starved for a week, although he looked far from starved! To say he was portly would be kind, with a red bulbous nose which suggested he enjoyed his drink as well as his food. The lack of hair on his head was made up for in the bushy moustache which danced on his top lip as his jaws worked on the food. What had I let myself in for? Rachel had really dropped me in it; taking advantage of the guilt trip I was on to lumber me with the uncle from hell. Still, I owed her, I would do my duty.

The speeches were over and the cake ceremoniously carved up and passed round. The guests were beginning to relax after the delicious food and drink and alas, it was time for me to fulfil my promise. The hotel staff were busily clearing the tables, making ready for the evening buffet and disco when I spotted Uncle Harry sitting alone at the side of the room. I breathed deeply pulling myself up to my full five foot three inch height and marched over. Fixing a smile on my face, I offered my hand to Harry.

"Hi, you must be Rachel's uncle, I'm Jayne..." I was about to ask how he was enjoying the wedding, when he opened his mouth and let out the most revolting belch, I had to resist the urge to turn and run, I did owe my friend.

"Better out than in, that. Aye lass, I'm Rachel's uncle and I was hoping to have a little chat with the prettiest bridesmaid I've ever seen!"

Yuk, gross... did I really have to talk to this man? Then I looked across at Rachel in her wheelchair, wistfully watching as her guests began to dance. Not for her the pleasure of leading the dancing with her new husband. Okay, it was only for a few hours so I obediently sat beside that hulk of a man as he patted the empty seat next to him.

It took less than two minutes of Uncle Harry's company for me to work out why he wasn't married, but what I couldn't for the life of me grasp was why Rachel had said he was her favourite uncle. But then she did say she hadn't seen him for ages. Harry had two pints of beer on the table in front of him. As he downed the first, in one gulp, I glanced again at Rachel. She smiled and gave me a little wave; I bravely smiled back, trying to look as if I was having fun. It was going to be a long night.

I caught Rachel looking at me a few times in the next twenty minutes or so and she seemed as if something was bothering her. She must be feeling awful being an observer to the dancing at her own wedding. When Harry excused himself to go back to the bar, I moved over to talk to her.

"Are you okay?" I asked, praying that nothing was wrong.

"Yes, but I hoped you'd be giving some of your attention to Uncle Harry." Rachel looked disappointed.

"I am" I replied, "He's only gone to get another drink."

"Oh no." Rachel began to shake with laughter, "That's not Harry, that's Uncle Jim, Gladys's husband. That's Harry over there." She pointed to the young man sitting in the far corner, studying the flowers on the wallpaper, the young man I had mistakenly thought to be Gladys's son.

"But he's not much older than you. How can he be your uncle?"

"He's mum's youngest brother, an afterthought as far as my grandparents were concerned. Did you really think I'd ask my best friend to babysit someone like Uncle Jim?"

I didn't know whether to laugh or cry. I should have known it wasn't in her nature to play a trick like that. Rachel took me over and introduced me to Harry. He was, thankfully, the complete opposite of Jim and as Rachel excused herself to return to Gareth, I sat beside Harry and the evening just got better and better. Underneath the shyness I found a kind, sensitive and interesting man. He loved his niece as I did, but we found we had much more in common. He was also rather gorgeous; I don't know why he hadn't been snapped up by some lucky girl.

I could hardly believe it was midnight, the evening had flown by in Harry's company, and I was beginning to wish it would never end. It was time for the bride and groom to say goodbye to their guests and head off to an unknown destination. As Harry and I made our way towards Rachel to wish her well, there was a flurry of activity and a rush of female guests heading towards the bride.

'Oh no' I thought, 'she's going to throw her bouquet.' I turned to move away from the throng, determined not to even attempt to catch it, mainly for fear of living with my mother if I did. She would be unbearable. I smiled at Harry as I turned, but his attention was distracted and before I could drag him away, Harry had caught the bouquet. A cheer went up, and his face turned crimson. In his embarrassment, he quickly passed the flowers to me.

When I eventually managed to see Rachel, she had a wicked grin on her face.

"What do you think of Uncle Harry?" It was only then that I realised I had been set up, but I didn't care in the slightest. I bent down to kiss my friend and said a quiet thank you.

"I can certainly see why he's your favourite uncle." I whispered.

The End

Poor Malcolm

Malcolm's mother was impressed with her teeth.

Malcolm had been brought up to respect women. In fact it would be true to say that Malcolm loved women.

At the tender age of eighteen he fell in love with Josie, a real looker, curves in all the right places, silky blonde tresses and baby blue eyes, the full package. Malcolm was hooked the first time he set eyes on her and gladly bought the ring when she suggested getting engaged. Within a year they were married. Opposition from his usually controlling mother hadn't been as strong as he expected, but mother liked Josie, who wouldn't?

Of course they had both been too young. Malcolm was happy, but Josie felt she had missed out on youth and freedom and one day Malcolm came home to a 'Dear John' letter. He was heartbroken having truly loved Josie, but his mother reminded him that there were plenty more fish in the sea.

Sally looked nothing like a fish. Another looker and she was interested in him, Malcolm couldn't believe his luck. Sally was a feisty red head with piercing green eyes which captivated him from the start. After a whirlwind romance they were married on a beach in St. Lucia, so romantic.

But Sally soon began to complain that Malcolm was dull, boring and they didn't go out any more. Malcolm tried his best to keep his new wife happy, but failed miserably. Sally left without so much as a note, although she did send a text telling him she had cleared out their joint bank account.

Helen wasn't what could be called a beauty but had very good teeth, Malcolm's mother was impressed with her teeth. Malcolm thought it was probably better to settle down with Helen rather than another flighty looker. It was a long courtship but Malcolm was in no hurry, it was a good omen that things were so different from his first two marriages, or so his mother said. The wedding was a registry office affair with only a handful of guests. Helen looked smart, perhaps Malcolm wished for a little more than smart, but he'd been down that road before. 'Third time lucky,' he told himself, settling down to domestic bliss. Malcolm was happy enough and thought Helen was too. But Helen was keeping a diary. She had noted all the ways in which Malcolm could improve. Every gift he had given, every compliment, every evening out was noted and graded on how satisfactory it had been. When Helen told him she was leaving, she showed him the diary and explained why. The 'Dear John' letter had been kinder.

Malcolm resolved to remain single. Three marriages were enough and quite exhausting. But when Davina moved in across the street from his mother's, Malcolm didn't stand a chance. She too had been married three times and was actively seeking husband number four. Davina quickly took over Malcolm's life, making all the arrangements. Malcolm just went with the flow. A trip to Gretna Green was Davina's idea of making them feel young again, and so she became wife number four after knowing Malcolm for only six months.

Davina was, like wife number one and two, a looker and Malcolm was smitten, desperately hoping this marriage would work; he really did enjoy being a husband, even if his track record proved he had little talent for the role. Davina seemed content, but Malcolm was never sure, never off his guard in case he messed up again. Davina loved to socialise, with Malcolm, with the girls from work, she was always game for a good night out. It was after one of her girlie outings that Malcolm noticed subtle changes towards him. He dreaded a text, a letter or a diary appearing, feeling once again a failure. Davina grew cool towards him; he was certain she would leave. But he was wrong. Davina didn't leave him. Early one Wednesday morning the police arrived at their front door. They asked several questions, which Malcolm answered truthfully before being arrested and led out of his own front door in handcuffs.

There was plenty of time for Malcolm to think about his stupidity as he waited in the holding cell for the sentence to be decided. As he was taken into the dock he could see Josie, Sally, Helen and Davina sitting together awaiting the judge's decision, all hoping that bigamy would bring a sentence of forever and a day, with the key thrown away.

The End

Chain Reaction

"I quite like it that just when I think I know you inside out, you can still surprise me!"
Jerry said.

"Please, please say you're not angry with me." Mel smiled into Jerry's eyes, her own baby blue ones giving a look she hoped he could not resist.

"Of course I'm not angry with you. It's just that we were going to save our money this year and have a proper holiday later." he replied, "But okay, I know these last few weeks have been difficult, perhaps you're right."

Mel wrapped her arms around Jerry's neck, kissing his cheek and breathing in the fragrance of sandalwood cologne. She had known he would understand which was just as well as she had already paid in full. Jerry grinned, then added,

"I quite like it that just when I think I know you inside out, you can still surprise me!"

He was right; booking the holiday had been totally out of character for Mel. She didn't do spontaneous. Generally her life was planned with an almost military precision, with days meticulously ruled by her diary, but hey, it had been a great last minute bargain and she really did feel in need of a holiday. Mel had been rushing around like a whirling Dervish these last few weeks looking after Gran, a job her mother usually took care of, but she was out of action with a broken arm. So with seeing to Gran's needs and helping mum out, she was exhausted but mum's plaster cast would come off later in the week and Mel felt she'd earned a bit of four star luxury.

"It'll be my birthday while we're away. Benidorm can be my present." Mel passed the brochure to her boyfriend hoping to inspire him with pictures of white sandy beaches and bright blue skies.

A week later the young couple were strolling along Benidorm beach, hand in hand on a gloriously hot day. Mel loved the silky feel of the warm sand between her toes and the smell of salty air mingled with sun cream. A light sea breeze cooled their skin as they sauntered along the stretch of powdery white sand in a carefree mood, Mel swinging her sandals by her side, almost skipping along beside Jerry.
"I knew this was a good idea." She chirped, still a little unsure that Jerry was as enthralled as her about the holiday.
"You were right love, Everything's perfect, the hotel, the food, the weather, you." He squeezed her hand and she relaxed, thinking how lucky she was to have such a thoughtful boyfriend.
The second day dawned as bright as the first. Mel threw back the curtains and opened the balcony door to look out on a magnificent view... of the dustbins! Jerry teased her about it, but it had been a cheap last minute deal and this was the only negative so far. Besides if you leaned over the balcony and twisted your head as far right as possible, there was a sea view. It was like glimpsing a sparkling sapphire reflecting the rays of the sun, a flash of nature's beauty beckoning to them beyond the dustbins. Who cared about the view? They rose early to get outside, determined to make the most of each moment.
Long, leisurely walks filled their daytime hours, helping to offset the effects of eating too much of the delicious Spanish cuisine served in the hotel. People watching became part of their routine, making up stories about strangers and inventing scenarios to explain their expressions. Many of the locals walked dogs, seeming to favour small breeds, which they treated like children. One

lady, wearing a bright pink knitted poncho had a cute little Chihuahua trotting alongside, wearing a matching pink coat with a tiny ribbon clipped to its head. Mel chuckled; she was a passionate animal lover.

The first few days were spent exploring the old part of Benidorm where Mel became fascinated with the steeply winding steps up to the 'Placa del Castell'. The square offered incredible views over the ocean and the tiny Isla de Benidorm which Jerry thought resembled a giant granite doorstop wedged into the sea. But it wasn't only the views which captivated her; it was the steps themselves, a shrine to lovers everywhere. A heavy metal chain-link rail ran up both sides of the stone steps and attached to almost every link were hundreds of padlocks of all sizes. Each one bore the names of lovers, some with a date and others with tender inscriptions. Many larger padlocks had small ones locked onto them, which Mel thought must be children whose names were added later as they arrived into the world. She spent ages reading names and fondling individual locks, trying to visualize faces to match the names and dreaming up romantic stories for each couple. Jerry occupied the time by counting as many locks as he could, but gave up as he neared a thousand, then he almost had to drag Mel away; being so fascinated by the chain and its significance. At the top of the steps the 'Placa del Castell' itself seemed a magical place. Set above the pretty little beach, 'Playa del Mal Pas', it was a popular spot for tourists.

A group of about twenty tourists came out of the Church, 'Placa De Sant Jaume', following a guide carrying a pole with a brightly coloured felt parrot on top. The party jostled to keep up and hear what she had to say as they made their way down 'El Callejon', a narrow cobbled street leading to the heart of the old town. Mel was enchanted with the square and was in no hurry to leave.

They examined the huge richly embossed brass doors of the Church, which must have been at least sixteen feet high, then ventured into the adjacent leather market."Don't you just love the smell of leather?" Mel stroked the exquisitely soft jackets on display. Jerry was pleased to see her so happy, thinking that this holiday had been a good idea after all. Stepping out into the bright sunshine, she immediately spotted something else to enthuse about.

"Oh look at those cats over there!"

Jerry turned to look at where she pointed and his eyes rested on an old lady carefully filling dishes with food and water, feeding a small colony of feral cats. After watching for a few minutes, they approached the woman to ask about the cats but she spoke no English. With gestures, smiles and nods, they eventually learned that six cats lived in the square and the old lady made the climb every day to feed them. Moving away Mel was touched by the lady's devotion.

"It's like the old lady in 'Mary Poppins' who feeds the birds at St. Paul's Cathedral!" Mel said.

An afternoon by the pool refreshed them after their long walk and the days began to take on the same leisurely pattern, walking each morning then swimming and sun-bathing during the hot afternoon hours.

One morning, as they were again drawn to 'Placa del Castell', Jerry paused at the foot of the stone steps and from his pocket produced a small padlock on which was written both their names. Mel squealed with delight,

"When did you get that?" Pleasure lit up her face.

"While you were lazing in bed and I nipped out for a paper."

Mel almost knocked him off his feet leaping into his arms, exactly the reaction he'd hoped for.

"You do know that I love you, don't you?" He asked.

Mel nodded, stunned into silence by such a romantic gesture.

"Well, now the whole world knows too." Jerry attached the padlock to the chain in a little gap near the bottom as Mel struggled to blink back tears.

It was the most perfect holiday that either of them could remember. The first ten days just flew over all too quickly, leaving only three more days to enjoy. Mel's birthday was the following morning but it could hardly get any better than their holiday had already been. Following their usual routine and intending to shop for a few gifts to take home, fate broke into their pattern and instead of spending the afternoon by the pool; they found themselves at the local hospital.

Jerry had been walking ahead through a shopping mall, when his foot slipped on the top of the marble tiled steps leading down to the next level. He fell the full length of the stairs, each one painfully jolting his back, until he landed awkwardly in a heap at the bottom, his right leg twisted beneath him. It happened so quickly with Mel watching helplessly as he banged his head on the last step to add to his misery.

The local shop keepers were marvellous; an ambulance was called for and they wouldn't let Jerry move until it arrived, a sensible precaution. In less than an hour they had been whisked away to hospital and Mel was holding his hand, feeling almost as bad as he did, waiting for the results of X-rays. Fortunately there were no broken bones but severe bruising to his spine, a badly twisted ankle and knee and a mild concussion.

"Might knock some sense into me," he joked feebly.

Mel stayed as long as the nursing staff allowed, then returned to a lonely hotel room to ring Jerry's parents and let them know what had happened. Naturally they were shocked, but relieved that there were no serious injuries.

"The hospital wants to keep him in until our flight home." She told them miserably.

After a restless night, Mel awoke to the same glorious weather they had come to expect.

"Happy birthday Mel." She spoke gloomily to an empty room.

Eating breakfast alone in the hotel dining room was an uncomfortable experience. The waiters enquired after Jerry and she told them about the accident. They rallied round to try to cheer her up, flirting mildly, then sending their good wishes as she left to go to the hospital.

Because Jerry was in a private room, Mel was able to stay with him for most of the day. He too had had an uncomfortable night, tossing and turning in pain and unable to settle.

"Happy birthday love!" he smiled, "It's not quite the way I thought we'd spend the day, but we'll have to make the best of it I suppose."

Mel tried to match his pragmatic attitude and hide her disappointment.

"How had you wanted to spend the day?" She asked.

"Well, to tell the truth, this is the second time I've been thwarted in my plans for your birthday."

She sat up, intrigued.

"I'd booked us a meal at 'The County'. I know how much you love it there, but then you sprung this holiday on me and I had to cancel."

"Oh Jerry, I'm so sorry…"

"Don't worry; it's been a great holiday, until now. Besides, it probably didn't cost as much as a meal at 'The County' would have."

"What's the second time? You said you'd been thwarted twice." Mel asked curious to know what they would have been doing if they hadn't been stuck in hospital.

"Ah well, I suppose I'm here until the flight home, so there's no chance for plan B now is there?"

"Plan B, what's that?" She was itching to know now.

"Come here and I'll tell you." He patted the side of the bed and as Mel sat next to him he wrapped his arms around her.

"Close your eyes and I'll tell you what we should have been doing today."

Mel closed her eyes, leaning back into his embrace, and Jerry began.

"Imagine it's after dark. The sky is like black velvet, and the stars are diamonds twinkling in it. It's warm and the air is still. The only noise is the sound of crickets dancing in the darkness and the gentle swell of the waves on the shore. We're walking down El Callejon over the same cobbles people have walked for centuries. At the bottom of the hill there's a little tapas bar, lit only by candlelight. The candles are in old wine bottles, hardly visible for the wax which has built up over time. The walls are solid stone, it feels as if we're in a cave, but it's not cold, just a welcome cool from the day's hot sun. The wine is rich and fruity and the food smells delicious. Are you hungry Mel? Keep your eyes closed."

"Mmn, I'm starving." Mel was transported into the bar and could almost feel the atmosphere as Jerry continued.

"Good. We'll have to wait a little while; the food is all freshly prepared. There's a Spanish guitar playing quietly somewhere nearby. We're the only customers tonight and you look radiant. I love that emerald green dress you wear, you look so beautiful Mel. But while we're waiting I want to give you your birthday present. I bought it a while ago and this is the moment I'd chosen to give it to you, here in this little restaurant." Jerry stopped talking and turned Mel around to face him.

"Open your eyes." He whispered. Jerry was holding a little silk box and her heart skipped a beat. He offered it to her and she slowly opened it. The ring was a simple solitaire on a delicate gold band, perfect for her small hands.

"Will you marry me?" he asked hopefully.

Mel's feelings were written all over her face, Jerry was confident of her answer.

"I'd be honoured to be your wife." She smiled through tears of joy, looking down at the ring, glittering like the stars in the sky.

The End

The steps leading to the Placa del Castell is an actual place in Benidorm and are flanked by a heavy chain filled with padlocks. Mel and Jerry's padlock can be found near the bottom on the right hand side.

London Lifestyles

As long as George had his health and strength he would provide for his family.

George worked six days a week to provide for his family and felt his pride in so doing was justified. Both daughters attended private schools and his wife, Sal, had the luxury of not working, except for the charities she deigned to give patronage to. George delighted in giving his 'girls' an enviable lifestyle; membership of an exclusive country club and accounts at Harrods and Harvey Nics were taken for granted. Seeing the designer clothes, shoes and handbags cluttering his daughters' bedrooms gave him a sense of satisfaction. He had vowed that his family would never go without, as he had done. Getting out of the deprived council estate of his childhood had been George's priority, ever since he learned the power which money could bring.... As long as George had his health and strength he would provide for his family, taking delight in their affluence.

The price George paid was in the long monotonous hours he worked, leaving the house most mornings before Sal and the girls were awake. Each day began the same, a solitary breakfast of orange juice, coffee and croissants, before George reversing his silver Lexus out from beside Sal's red Peugeot convertible, slip it into gear and weave through the quiet early morning streets to the underground station. A near-by lock up garage proved more economical than paying the exorbitant congestion charges in the city and George parked the Lexus and walked to the tube station. His day had begun.

****

Victoria underground heaved with early morning commuters. Blasts of hot air swirled around corners, carrying odours, pleasant and not so pleasant, as people from all walks of life rubbed shoulders and breathed in the same stale air.

Tapping his stick along the tiled walls, the blind man kept close to the side. His dark glasses shielded him from the stares of passers-by and he ignored the jostling crowd, making his way to his usual, most profitable spot. Pulling his two dirty overcoats around his frame, for comfort rather than warmth, he eased himself down, took a cloth bag from his pocket, extracted a harmonica and began to play, placing the bag on the floor to receive the day's takings.

There were times when the beggar had been spat upon and had obscenities shouted at him, but for the most part people were generous, especially if they had witnessed such abuse. At the end of the day, the rhythmic tap-tapping of his stick was heard echoing through the underground as he reversed the journey, heavily weighted down with loose change from hundreds of commuters.

****

George unlocked the garage door, slipped inside and closed it behind him. He deftly shed the skin of the blind beggar, removing the dark glasses and the wig and locking them away with the two overcoats and white stick. The Lexus engine purred into life and George smiled to himself as he headed home to his family, satisfied with another day's work.

The End

The Postman's Daughter

She would be the Florence Nightingale of the modern age.

When Kate was nine years old she finally realised that her lifelong ambition of being a princess was more than likely never going to happen. The day arrived when she just had to accept the fact that there was a severe shortage of princes to marry, and even kissing a frog was unlikely to fulfil those childhood dreams. It was a hard lesson to learn for a little country girl and her disappointment was compounded as her tenth birthday approached and she found out that Santa Claus didn't really exist.

"Never mind love." Her father's voice was soothing, "You'll always be my princess...and don't tell your mother but Santa is my middle name."

Kate chuckled; she adored her father and liked nothing more than to accompany him on his rounds, a treat which was only allowed during school holidays. In her young and dreamy eyes, being the village postman was the most important job in the world, after being a princess of course. People were always pleased to see the postman, and when he gave them their letters, she could sense their excitement and anticipation. Her father had to curb her curiosity on more than one occasion, when she couldn't resist asking who the letter was from and what was inside. But no-one minded, Kate was a lovely girl, both inside and out and the villagers thought it a special treat for themselves, as well as her, when she was with her father.

Her tenth birthday passed, as did her eleventh and twelfth and it seemed like only a twinkling of an eye before Kate was a young woman. She still accompanied her father on his round whenever possible, walking through their village chatting companionably, then driving out to the farms and neighbouring villages. Still a dreamer, Kate felt like the luckiest girl in the world. Her ambitions had come and gone with the seasons; one day she wanted to be a vet, pulling on her green wellies and braving all weathers to treat a sick calf and its mother. Then she took a fancy for being an air hostess, travelling to exotic places, having a permanent tan and flirting with the pilots. And there was a time she decided to be a barrister, picturing herself in a smart black pencil skirt, low heeled black patent shoes, a flowing gown and a wig. Kate would make a name for herself defending the innocent, righting wrongs and seeking justice for the underdog. But then there was nursing; a crisp white dress pinched into her tiny waist by a silver buckle, black stocking and sensible shoes...she would be the Florence Nightingale of the modern world, dispensing compassion with medication and holding the hands of her patients to pass on her courage and fortitude. Teaching was another fleeting ambition. She simply knew she could inspire and enthuse the young, making learning fun and passing on her love of life and quest for knowledge.

As she dreamed her dreams Kate became more and more confused. Having done well in her 'A' levels the teachers encouraged her to apply for the top universities, proud of their postman's daughter who had the ability to go far.

Acceptance at Oxford was celebrated by the whole community; no-one from their village had ever gone to Oxford. Kate was both excited and terrified by the prospect. How would she cope living in a big city and knowing not a soul? Her whole life had been enveloped by the love of people she knew... who knew her and were like family.

It seemed as if the whole village came to see her off at the station, it was quite overwhelming. Hugs and good wishes were flung about like confetti and many eyes sparkled with tears. Kate was proud, yet sad to be leaving. Who would keep Dad company now, or run errands for old Mrs Simmons down the street? Would her mother miss her as much as she would miss her mother? And would Mother have the time to take the dogs out and clean the rabbit hutch?

Oxford was magnificent. Kate's eyes grew wide, dancing at every new sight. She loved the intricate architecture and the history they told, the busyness of the streets, the constant ringing of bicycle bells, and the crush of people. Such a contrast from village life. Kate was determined to work hard and make her family proud. She joined a book club, signed up for rowing lessons, volunteered to write for the student union news sheet and even squeezed in a part time job on two evenings a week, waitressing in a trendy bistro in the heart of the city.

Lectures were something else. Kate never missed a single one in the first term, soaking up the history of modern art, the romance of ancient Greece, and the psychology of contemporary man. Her interests had no bounds, there was nothing she found boring and her mind positively buzzed with the wonderful new world she was living in. Other students found her zest for life attractive and were drawn to Kate like moths to a flame. She seemed to fit at least thirty hours into every twenty four and was an inspiration to fellow students and a delight to the tutors.

The first chance to travel back home to the Scottish Borders was at Christmas, having used the half term break to work extra hours and complete assignments. By the time she saw her family again there was so much to tell them. An early snow was on the hills; the forecast was for a long hard winter but Kate was up and dressed by 6am on the first morning home, even after talking with her parents late into the night before.

"Goodness me." Her Father was surprised to see Kate up so early, "We thought you'd be wanting a lie in, you must be tired."

"But I've so wanted to get out on the round with you Dad. I've missed our times together." So father and daughter set off like old times, bundled up against the sharp wind and the threatening sleet. Her breath was white and the tip of her nose red as their boots scrunched on the thick early morning frost. Kate had become used to the milder weather of Oxford but there was something cleansing and healthy about a good crisp morning.

It was on that first morning's round that Kate began to realise that all was not well. Her Dad was as jolly as ever but somehow slower, pausing to catch his breath more often than before. Later she would ask Mother about it, but for now she was glad to be there to help him.

"Oh, it's just old age catching up." Mother laughed off Kate's concern. "We're none of us getting any younger."

The first year at uni positively flew over. Her lively mind was equal to all the challenges set before her and she was happy and content in this new exciting life. As expected, the second and third years brought more rigorous challenges academically but nothing with which Kate felt out of her depth. The finals drew near and although there was that nervous flutter in her stomach at the anticipation of the end of her course, she had no great fears and the tutors were predicting an excellent degree. The dreamer in her had still not decided on a career while fellow students had made their plans, some even having secured jobs. Kate changed her mind almost daily, knowing she would recognise her future career at some point but even she had to admit that time was running out.

News from home was always welcome and her parents often rang the house she shared with three other girls. The phone call early one May morning was, however, unwelcome news. Kate's father had suffered a stroke and was in the intensive care unit in Carlisle. It was, of course, a huge shock; since that first year away she had begun to see her parents more objectively and as her mother had pointed out, they were not getting any younger. But Kate had certainly not been prepared for this. Her mother begged her not to rush straight home knowing that the finals were underway but Kate simply had to go. A free weekend, which had been set aside for revision gave the opportunity to catch the first train north and head straight to the hospital.

It is often at such difficult times that people realise how fortunate they are if they have never come close to losing a loved one and that is just how she felt. One of her house-mates had lost her mother during their second year and Kate had experienced second hand how devastating such loss could be but now it was way too close to home. She couldn't bear the thought of losing her beloved father and when she entered the tiny hospital room, seeing him wired up to various monitors and tubes and looking so grey and ill, it was difficult to hold herself together. He was unconscious, but she still kissed him and whispered to him before embracing her mother whom she had never seen looking so strained and tired. Later, her mother was to say that Kate's presence was the turning point in her husband's recovery. A fact which could not be ignored as from that weekend he seemed to find the strength to fight his way back to health. Kate returned to Oxford knowing that he was on the way to recovery and able to complete her finals with a lighter heart.

The village heard the news of Kate's success in getting a first from Oxford and celebrated as if it was a national holiday. She received flowers, cards, homemade jams, chocolates and even a kitten as gifts. Although life at uni had been an exciting adventure and she had loved every minute, Kate was overjoyed to be home again. Her father had taken early retirement, insisted upon by her mother, so there were to be no more early morning rounds together. Kate knew that she could no longer dream of what she would do in life; it was now time to get on and do it.

Strangely, the desire she had once had to travel to exotic places had evaporated and the one certainty in her mind was that she wanted to stay in the village. It was home; she had experienced the excitement of university but now craved her roots and her own people. The only reminder of those fanciful childhood dreams was the kitten's name, Princess.

The position of librarian had just become available in the nearby town, a post which appealed to Kate and for which she was ideally suited. The interview was a formality, Kate was more than qualified, but her talents would not be wasted as the position included implementing a complete overhaul of the library with the introduction of a computer suite, a challenge she would relish.

There were some who had expected Kate would fill her father's shoes, delivering the mail, but that position had already been taken. Graham was from the next village, a tall sandy haired young man whose physique suggested a love of the outdoor life. His twinkling green eyes crinkled as he laughed; a sound which could be heard regularly from the new postman. On Kate's day off, she fell into the habit of rising early as she had always done, and setting off to walk through the village. It seemed the most natural thing in the world for her to fall into step with Graham; her feet walked that route automatically. The locals smiled and nodded their knowing looks and approval, anticipating the joy of a wedding in their midst, when the postman's daughter would become the postman's wife.

The End

The Interview

It was strange how her dreams always bore an affinity to a 'Mills and Boon' storyline.

Ellen walked to the edge of the diving board and paused before making her dive, looking out beyond the hotel grounds to the shimmering sapphire blue of the Mediterranean Sea. The heat of the sun warmed her golden, tanned body and Ellen smiled, aware of appreciative eyes upon her, particularly from the male guests at the hotel. Flexed feet, raised arms, she was poised to dive into the cooling water, when an unbearably loud burst of ringing made her cover her ears with her hands. Ellen rolled over and groped for the alarm clock.

"Why did I have to set it so early?" she thought, then instantly remembered; the job interview. Ellen struggled out from under the duvet and made her way to the bathroom. She always seemed to wake up just as her dreams were getting interesting, missing what could well be a fantastic ending. Would she have made a spectacular dive and been applauded by the onlookers, envious of her skill and grace? Would she have injured herself (only slightly of course,) necessitating a dramatic rescue from a handsome lifeguard? Or, horror of horrors, would her bikini strap have snapped, resulting in an extremely embarrassing moment? In real life, the latter would almost certainly be the most likely scenario.

It was strange how her dreams always bore an affinity to a 'Mills and Boon' storyline. In them she appeared to be at least six inches taller and considerably slimmer, as if someone had squeezed upwards from her ankles, redistributing all the chunky bits and moulding them into a perfect size ten. If only! Ellen's thoughts reluctantly turned to the morning interview. She had ironed her new blouse the evening before; it was smart, feminine, crisp white, with just the right amount of ruffles at the neck. Ideal to set off her business suit, or it would have been if she hadn't been daydreaming and scorched it; yet another expensive duster.

For Ellen this interview was a necessary evil, she had only ever had one job since leaving college, bookkeeping for a local mini-mart. But the owner was retiring soon and sadly the store would close. Spotting the job vacancy at 'Goodfellow and Son' solicitors, she had nervously applied and now found herself dreading what the morning would bring. Ellen was so painfully shy that even mixing socially was a chore and at any event she did attend, became the traditional wallflower. Her perception of herself was that of a dull, entirely uninteresting human being. Consequently Ellen dressed to fit that image, her wardrobe consisting of black and grey clothes, without any vibrant colours at all, being short and pear shaped, why would she draw attention to herself? And her hair, oh how she hated that frizzy red hair, and if she had once had hopes of growing out of the freckles…well at twenty-six it now looked extremely unlikely.

Finishing breakfast, Ellen dragged herself upstairs to dress, where looking in the mirror was a stark reminder of last night's other disaster. Having felt a little girlie pampering might boost her confidence, an idea all the best magazines subscribed to, she had attempted to pluck her eyebrows, realising all too late that she should have worn her glasses to do so. Not getting them quite even, Ellen had plucked more… and more, until now it appeared she had almost no brows at all. And it had been painful too, but at least they didn't look quite as red as they had last night. Finally, she was ready.

Stepping off the bus in the Market Place, Ellen groaned as she felt her heel slipping into a grate. Stuck fast, there was no alternative but to take off the offending shoe and yank it out with both hands.

"Oh no!" she cried watching the shoe come away from its heel, and to top it all the heel dropped into the drain, there was no way of retrieving that. Aware of passers-by smiling at her dilemma, she quickly put on the shoe and with no time to buy another pair, limped bravely on.

The office was on the first floor and Ellen, aware of the uneven clipperty clopping as she climbed the stairs, found herself in a small, well lit and comfortable reception area where a motherly receptionist smiled, such a warm friendly smile, it made her want to cry. Ellen tried to explain her strange gait and was rewarded with another encouraging smile.

"Sit down dear and I'll see if Mr. Goodfellow's ready for you."

Taking a few deep breaths in a futile effort to calm herself, Ellen could feel her face burning when the receptionist returned.

"He'll see you now, this way dear. If you try walking on the ball of your foot I shouldn't think he'll even notice."

Ellen dutifully followed, wobbling slightly in an effort to walk evenly. The receptionist squeezed her arm as she left the room, closing the door to leave Ellen alone, facing a potential new employer. He rose from his seat, knocking over a mug of coffee from the desk as he did so. Ellen watched as Mr. Goodfellow floundered, not knowing quite what to do, and was amused to see that he was actually blushing.

"Here, let me help" she offered, picking up the cup and pulling a packet of tissues from her bag to mop up the excess coffee.

"There's not much, I don't think it will stain the carpet. I always carry these," Ellen waved the packet of tissues.

"I'm rather accident prone myself." Placing the soggy tissues in the bin, she stood to look at the man before her. This was obviously the 'and son' half of the partnership, Ellen had expected to see the senior Mr. Goodfellow.

"Ppp…lease sit down," he offered a chair.

"Ssss…orry about tthat, clumsy of me." Young Mr. Goodfellow then launched into an obviously prepared speech, explaining how his father now only worked part time and their receptionist, Mrs Cummins, who'd been with them forever, was retiring. Ellen nodded, hopefully in all the appropriate places.

'He's nervous,' she thought, 'talking too quickly, fiddling with papers on the desk, blushing; a classic case of shyness,' and she should know. As Ellen looked into young Mr. Goodfellow's eyes, she sighed, no longer hearing the rehearsed words, she was transported back to a shimmering, sapphire Mediterranean Sea.....

Outside the office door, Mrs Cummins listened unashamedly to the interview in progress, delight growing within at everything she heard. She had known her young employer since he was a boy and knew how painfully shy he could be, but there was something about this girl, she seemed like an ideal match. Ooh, it was just like one of the romances in the 'Mills and Boon' books she loved so much! Hopefully this was one young couple who would almost certainly live happily ever after.

The End

It's all in thePlanning.

Dad would have been proud of me today.

The rain lashed down on the windscreen, blurring the darkening road ahead. I didn't care; I was ecstatic, the adrenalin was pulsing through my veins. The wipers worked furiously to clear the rain and I couldn't wait to get home and raise a glass in memory of my old Dad who had taught me everything I know.
"It's all in the planning Michael," he would instruct. "Planning and preparation, then you'll be successful my boy."

I smiled at the memory, remembering how I'd worshiped everything about him. I longed to grow up and work with him; to be at the top of the tree as he was. People had respect for my Dad. No-one crossed him, not even Mam. She knew which side her bread was buttered. I could remember him lifting me up on his shoulders and striding down to the corner shop.
"Anything you fancy Mikey boy, and it's yours." He would laugh as I dithered over what to choose; gob-stoppers, black bullets, sherbet fountains, everything a boy could wish for and my Dad, holding my hand. Life couldn't get any better than this. Then there were the hours we spent in the garden shed. Dad's collection fascinated me and if he was in a good mood he would let me sort through his 'tools'. Tiny screwdrivers, bits of wire, old padlocks, torches, things to fascinate any boy. Mam would get cross when he took me out there.
"Leave the boy alone Jack." She would plead. "Let him make his own way in life." But Dad always had the last word; I was to be trained as he had been, he told Mam and that was all I had ever wanted .Dad would have been

proud of me today. I'd been meticulous in the planning and execution of this job, one of my biggest so far. A pretty fair day's work all round. Weeks and weeks I've watched that supermarket, cost me a fortune in coffees too but it was a brilliant plan, so easy.

Creatures of habit in these supermarkets, they deserve to get robbed, even a child could think up better security than they had.
Just a few more miles and then I can really celebrate, now where did I put those fags? Hell's bells, what was that?

****

I can see him now. He looks much smaller in here and the smiles are gone too, he was cross with Mam.
"Why d'you have to bring the lad?" He scowled at her and ignored me.
"He wanted to come Jack; you know how he idolises you." But Dad seemed different somehow. Gone was the confident proud man I knew. He'd lost weight and there were dark circles under his eyes. He wore an ill-fitting boiler suit of kinds, not the dapper man I knew and looked up to. Mam had told me that there'd been some sort of mistake and Dad had to go away for a while. I must have worn her down begging to go with her to visit him, and now I was wishing I'd never asked, it was making him cross. But Dad relented and pulled me onto his knee. Everything was fine again until I asked when he'd be coming home.
"It'll be a long time yet lad, so you'd better be good for your Mam and look after her for me."

I nodded my head, not daring to speak for fear of the hot tears I was holding back escaping.

****

I struggled to open my eyes but couldn't focus properly. It was dark, pitch black, and I was sprawled at an angle across the dash board of the car. The rain had stopped, I don't know how long I'd been unconscious, could be minutes or even hours. My head hurt, but even worse was the excruciating pain in my left leg. I reached down to touch it and felt a warm sticky fluid; blood! Outside was quiet and black as the grave. I could remember hitting something in the road, a fox or a rabbit perhaps and then swerving off down the bank. Bloody hell, I could be here all night! So dizzy...and the pain...

****

I cried all the way home. Mam tried to comfort me but I thought I would never see Dad again. People kept staring at us on the bus.
"Sshh Michael. It's bad enough that we have to go an' visit that place without you drawing attention to us now. Quiet son, please." But I couldn't help it. My Dad was no longer in charge. He had been led away by two big, burly guards who seemed intent on hurting him. They didn't need to be so rough. If he'd met them on the street he would have shown them who was boss. What mistake was it I wondered and why did Dad have to stay in that awful place?
Mam looked at me solemnly.
"Michael, your Dad's a villain." She had said before we set off, "There's no two ways about it. He's broken the law and now he has to do his time. Just let this be a lesson

to you, you're a bright boy, you can go places an' have a good life. Don't be like your Dad."

But all I'd ever wanted was to be like my Dad, he was my hero. I was eight years old and my Dad was my life. How could I not want to be like him?

****

Damn it. I must stay awake but it's so cold... got to get out of here and get help. How could it have gone so horribly wrong? I've always maintained that planning and preparation were essential for success and I'm usually right...oh...the pain's killing me! I couldn't have done much more to prepare but....sod it...there's only one way out now and everything I've worked for will be lost.

At least that bloody rain's stopped. I'll have to get out of the car but the pain's so bad, I feel weak and dizzy. It's dark too, pitch black but I can't complain at that, part of the plan that was.

It's laughable really, emptying the tills every hour at the same time and Securicor, never there before 5.00pm. An open invitation to anyone with half a mind, easy pickings; but hell, what a mess I'm in now, blood everywhere... must do something quickly.

Oh the look on that supervisor's face. Priceless! I'm sure she must have wet herself when I held the knife against her ribs.

"Just be a good girl and I won't have to use it." She'll be dreaming of me forever. And all that lovely cash, it's refreshing to know that in this world of the little plastic card so many people still use good old fashioned cash; dirty, crinkled notes, just how I like them. But what on earth can I do now? Perhaps if I hadn't driven so fast, or lit that cigarette?

The getaway was perfect, just as I planned. 4.20pm to get the maximum of the day's takings and miss the tea-time rush. The light would be fading then too, an hour's drive through the quiet country lanes, and I'd be home and dry. It could have worked like a dream; it should have worked like a dream. Sod's law I suppose. The bend was slippery with the rain. Thought I was a goner when I went off the road, reckon I still could be if I don't get this stupid door open.

The disguise was good, would have even fooled my old Mam, God bless her. A false beard works wonders and with the baseball cap and baggy charity shop track suit, I hardly recognised myself. Easy to whip off too, a quick strip in the car and I was back to a younger fitter man. The limp was a stroke of genius, trailing my leg and stooping forward; added twenty years at least.

Great, the doors open at last. A bit of mud won't hurt, not like this leg. I can't stand on it and the bone's sticking out. Bloody hell, if I don't get on with it I could pass out. No one can see me down here. Must attract attention quickly, I'm feeling quite light headed...

The car's a write off. A new car was the first thing on the wish list... this isn't turning out as I planned.

Ah, look at these lovely stuffed carriers. Wonder how much cash is in there. A holiday in the sun, a trip to LA, some new threads to impress the ladies, I'll never know.

Pull yourself together Michael; you have to do this. It's dark now, think. What options are left? Bleed to death in the mud and be found in a week's time, maybe a month? Or attract attention.

What would you have done Dad? I've always tried to think like you. You were the best in the game; I've tried so hard to be like you. What was that mistake which ended it all? I never did find out. Mam was tight lipped when I asked her. I only saw you one more time before...

...bad luck ending up in there and to die so young. Life's not fair, but you always told me that didn't you?

I wish we could have worked together. There would have been no mistakes then eh? More fun too. Jack and Mikey, just like you said it would be. You would have had a right good laugh today Dad. Those scared faces, grovelling to give me the money they were. A right good laugh we'd have had together.

Funny, can't feel the damn leg now, gone numb it has. Maybe the mud's good for it.

Hell, everything's soaked.

Attract attention Michael boy. You know what has to be done even if you weren't a boy scout. Sorry Dad, I didn't plan for this hiccup and it was going so well... attention, in the dark, it'll have to be a fire. Huh, a fire in a cold wet copse where everything is soaked. Just my luck that the only thing not sodden with this damned awful rain is my lovely crinkly cash! Gives new meaning to the phrase 'money or your life' eh? What would you do Dad? Only one thing to do really, it's a no win situation; keep the money and probably die, or burn the money and live... Where the hell are those matches?

The End

The Desk

It was to be their 'forever home' where they planned to bring up a family and grow old together.

Simon was abroad again and Jenny was missing him, even though he had only left yesterday. To be fair he did keep these business trips to a minimum and since their wedding nearly five years ago, he had never been away for more than a week at a time. This trip was to Los Angeles, the city of angels; a destination Jenny would dearly have loved to share with him, but her own business commitments were heavy at this time of year and it was impossible to get away. Still, he rang each evening, which brightened her day and a week wasn't really that long. Absence makes the heart grow fonder, not that Jenny could love him anymore than she already did. Five years had flown by and there was still that same flutter of excitement when hearing his voice on the phone or his key in the lock as there had been in the first few weeks of their relationship, that special 'getting to know each other' stage.

Today, Jenny had unexpectedly found herself with a free afternoon due to a client cancelling an appointment at the last minute. Returning to the office after lunch would have been the sensible thing to do, it wasn't as if she had no work to get on with but she thought a couple of hours shopping might be just the thing to lift her mood and she did want to look for an anniversary gift for Simon, a good enough reason to grasp this sudden opportunity.

Traditionally, the fifth wedding anniversary was known as the wooden one and Jenny knew what would be the ideal present for Simon. After their wedding, the couple had moved into a magnificent, albeit run down, Victorian house which they had lovingly restored and refurbished over the past five years. The kitchen and bathrooms were bang up to date, but for the large reception rooms they wanted to recreate the period splendour of the house and trawled antique shops for the right fireplaces, light fittings and occasional pieces of furniture. Their care and attention to detail had paid off giving them an absolutely stunning home, envied by their friends and loved by themselves. As often happens with such projects, they spent far more than they had originally budgeted for, but they both had good jobs, and it was to be their 'forever home' where they planned to bring up a family and grow old together.

Simon had a study on the ground floor of the house. The room had been decorated in keeping with the rest of the property, but the furniture lacked the character needed to complete the feel. His desk was a modern glass design which stuck out like a sore thumb but Simon had put off buying a more fitting one, saying they had already been extravagant and it could be replaced at a later date. Jenny had other ideas, an antique wooden desk would make the ideal anniversary present and so today she began to revisit some of the places they had discovered on previous shopping expeditions.

Antique shops seem to spring up in clusters, which Jenny always found odd but certainly convenient. In the pretty market town where they lived, the shops were on both sides of a steep bank, small curious places with tiny rooms crammed full of history. One or two, they had learned, were ridiculously expensive, so she avoided those, going into the ones she knew to hold the kind of treasure she was seeking yet after two hours Jenny had nothing to show for her pains except laddered tights from stepping over and around all manner of furniture. The only helpful thing to come out of the afternoon was the information from one kindly shop keeper that a forthcoming sale at a nearby auction house might have exactly the kind of desk she was looking for. There was still time to dash to the saleroom and pick up a catalogue, so she made that her last stop for the day before returning home.

Jenny had never been to an auction before and was unsure how it operated. The showroom was still open for viewing, so she stepped inside and began to wander around, immediately struck by the sheer volume of goods that had been crammed into the premises, not that there was any shortage of space. The showroom was an old church with a high ceiling and a gallery and every inch of space had been utilised, with furniture crammed into every nook and cranny and trestle tables weighted down with china, silverware, glassware and ornaments of every description. Boxes of assorted lots were underneath the tables and plenty of prospective buyers were rummaging through them. It would have been easy to get distracted, so Jenny steered herself away from the tables, concentrating on the furniture. Completing a circuit of the downstairs lots, she was becoming slightly disheartened. Only two desks were on display, neither of which appealed at all. Climbing the stairs to the gallery offered nothing new and Jenny was just about to turn and head for home when a gentleman approached, asking if he could help.
"I'm looking for a period desk," she told him, "but you don't seem to have many."
The man smiled and showed her through to an even larger room at the back, a warehouse filled with furniture of every age and description. Left alone to browse, Jenny found one that would fit the bill exactly. It would look amazing in the study... and the smile on Simon's face when he saw it. The catalogue described the desk as early 18th century, burr walnut gentleman's kneehole desk of the Queen Anne period, 1702 – 1714. Jenny ran her

fingers over the beautiful patina of the wood; it was in remarkable condition for its age, with five deep drawers and a large central cupboard and the ticket boasted the original pear drop handles and keys! Okay, it wasn't Victorian, but it was just the sort of desk a Victorian gentleman would have used. She had to have it, Simon would love it! On her way out, Jenny checked the details of the auction, only two days away, and learned that she must register to bid and the guide price was a whopping £3,500! Still she wasn't deterred, knowing it was an extravagance but it would be a once in a lifetime purchase and she was positive it was the right one for Simon. Heading home the excitement lifted the previous mood as she pictured the magnificent desk and her husband working at it.

The day of the auction arrived and Jenny was as keen as ever to buy the desk, although a little anxious about bidding. The auction room was buzzing with anticipation, packed to capacity and already in full swing. She squeezed into a tiny space at the back, waiting for the desk to be auctioned. At first, Jenny was afraid to move, thinking that a nod or a scratch of her nose might be interpreted as a bid. But she soon relaxed and even began to enjoy the proceedings, watching the auctioneer skilfully conduct the sale. Like the conductor of an orchestra, his hands moved deftly, picking out each bidder at remarkable speed. The desk was in the latter half of the sale and she became increasingly nervous as they moved swiftly through the lots. It was amazing how the auctioneer kept track of the bids. All the lots had been on the internet and there were people bidding on line and on the telephone. Jenny hoped there wasn't too much interest in the desk.

At last it was lot 2271, the beautiful desk! Jenny had realised that she shouldn't go straight in with a high bid and sure enough the auctioneer asked for a starting bid of

£3,000. There was a few moments silence; she was biting her tongue to hold herself back.

"Okay," the auctioneer scanned the room, "Start me at 2,000"

The man beside him on a laptop raised his hand and the bids had started. A woman in a white coat at the other side of the room raised her registration number and Jenny quickly did the same. The auctioneer pointed first to the lady, then Jenny, then back to the laptop man and then a telephone bid came in. Jenny was panicking; she couldn't lose the desk, but the bids were coming in, in hundreds of pounds. At £3,500 the lady in white shook her head and Jenny smiled. The man on the phone also shook his head and she dared to hope the desk was hers.

The laptop man raised his hand, so Jenny did the same...again the laptop...again Jenny. She was physically trembling now, having bid far more than she'd intended. At £4,000 she raised her hand, deciding that this would be her last bid. The laptop man shook his head and the auctioneer said those wonderful words,

"Sold to the lady at the back, for £4,000"

Jenny was trembling, with excitement or dread she wasn't sure, as she made her way through the crowds and into the office in the foyer to pay for her purchase, convinced that it was worth every penny. Delivery would be the next day; it would be in place when Simon arrived home.

By the day her husband was due to return home, Jenny had polished the desk until it shone. She only had a few brief pangs of regret at the price she had paid, but decided not to tell Simon of her extravagance, hoping he wouldn't ask. The airport was, as usual, hectic, but she finally saw her husband heading towards her and was soon enfolded in his arms, enjoying the comforting feel of his presence again. Jenny could hardly wait to show him the desk, barely giving him time to drop his luggage in the hall before making him close his eyes so she could lead him through to the study.

"You can open them now." she smiled, and was rewarded by the look of joy on Simon's face.

"It's magnificent!"

Jenny accepted another long hug, hoping he wouldn't ask the price.

Simon was obviously thrilled with the desk. He examined it closely, opening all the drawers in turn, enjoying the feel of the polished wood and grinning like a schoolboy with a new toy. Jenny need not have worried about him asking the price, her husband had no intention of asking how much she had paid and resolved that he never would. You see, he already knew, for he too had been at the very same auction, not in person, but virtually, as he placed his bids on the internet.

The End

Imagination?

There was something about a daisy chain; it seemed to represent all the innocence of childhood.

Mary listened to the happy chatter of her granddaughter and smiled. The little girl was having a really good natter with an imaginary friend and looked so happy. Her daughter came into the lounge carrying two cups of steaming coffee, gave one to her mother and settled on the sofa with the other.

"Lizzie's still got her little friend then." Mary remarked.

"Yes" Jill replied with a sigh. "I often wish she hadn't. She wants to play with him all the time and he has to come everywhere with us. I could get quite jealous... if he was real."

"So it's a little boy then is it? You had an imaginary friend too you know. Can you remember?"

"Vaguely, but it was only a passing phase, Lizzie's friend seems to have become a permanent lodger."

"Yours was a little girl called Tilly and every time anything was broken or lost it was always Tilly's fault, not yours. You used to tell everyone that she was your sister which I always felt was wishful thinking. Your Dad and I would have loved another child but it just didn't seem to happen..."

Jill put her hand over her mothers and squeezed it affectionately."I know Mum, and you were such wonderful parents it seems such a shame, but I got the benefit of having you and Dad all to myself!" With a distant look in her eyes Jill continued, "Dad would have loved Lizzie wouldn't he?"

Mary hardly needed to answer, Frank had doted on Jill and would most certainly have adored his granddaughter!

"Lizzie's friend isn't actually a little boy; I think he must be almost grown up. You should see her walking around with 'him', reaching up high to hold his hand. We must look quite comical walking down the street Lizzie holding my hand, with her other one high in the air."

"It'll pass love, she's only five and it does no harm, in fact such an imagination is good for a child of her age."

Jill sipped her coffee and almost as if to demonstrate the fact, Lizzie came running up, one arm reaching high in the air, to announce that she and her friend were going into the garden to play. When Mary had finished the coffee she left Jill preparing lunch and wandered outside to find Lizzie. The little girl was picking daisies from the lawn and passing them to her friend.

"Look Grandma!" she held out a chain of daisies, "My friend showed me how to do a necklace."

Mary took the chain from her granddaughter, threading it round her fingers as she thought. There was something about a daisy chain; it seemed to represent all the innocence of childhood. It felt like only yesterday that Jill was playing in just the same way herself.

"Does your friend have a name?" She asked.

"No, he's just my friend. I love him and he loves me."

Mary's eyes were suddenly moist as she watched this beautiful child playing so contentedly, secure in the love of her family, and without a care in the world.

After lunch, the child, mother and grandmother walked to the park where Lizzie could expend some of her youthful energy and they could all enjoy the late autumn sunshine which struggled to break out from behind fluffy white clouds. It was one of those days which made Mary feel good to be alive; they had done nothing special, except to enjoy each other's company, three generations in compatible harmony.

Back at home Jill brought out an old box of photographs she had been sorting through.

"There are some really ancient photos here Mum, I'd hoped you would go through them and fill in some of the names of people I don't recognise."

Mary was happy to oblige and was soon lost in the past, leafing through images of herself and her family which Jill's grandmother had passed on to her, some of which must have been fifty years old at least. Carefully marking the backs with a soft pencil, she began to place the photos in chronological order. It wasn't long before Jill and Lizzie joined her, giggling over the dated fashions and stern expressions of some of their ancestors. Lizzie didn't recognize her grandmother as a young woman or even photos of her mother as a child, but suddenly, with great excitement she picked up a photograph of a young man in military dress and announced to the room,

"Here's a picture of my friend! Where did you get this Mummy? It's him, look, look Granny!"

Mary and Jill were astonished as they did look, at the photograph of Lizzie's grandfather as a young soldier, in the prime of his life...

The End

Happy New Year

'How to Achieve a New, Improved You.'

Being woken at five thirty am on New Year's morning was not in my master plan or on my list of New Year resolutions, although Lucy, my cat, didn't seem to know this. It wouldn't normally have been a problem except that I'd only gone to bed at two am, but how could a hairball know that? And it could certainly have been worse as the offending hairball was deposited on my bedroom carpet mere inches away from my new fluffy pink slippers, an extravagant Christmas present from me to me, to mark the new improved Alicia; absolutely no more slovenly attire to be worn at any time, which included my ancient comfy moccasins, which now adorned the bin.

Scrubbing the bedroom carpet with foam cleaner, hot water and elbow grease had the effect of waking me up completely with a sharp aroma, akin to smelling salts I suspect and I knew it was useless to attempt going back to sleep. I would use the time efficiently, after all, getting up earlier had been on my list, although maybe not quite this early. The reasoning behind that particular resolution was to give myself time to eat a nutritious breakfast rather than running out of the house last minute and grabbing a donut and skinny latte to go. Being New Year's day I was not going to work of course but I determined to use the time constructively and rummaged around to find my new best friend, a copy of the much acclaimed book by Melissa-Jayne Fosdyke, 'Be Your Own Life Coach' subtitled, 'How to Achieve a New, Improved You.' My sister had oh so kindly bought the book and given it to me well before the festive season, assuring me that I would find Christmas so much easier if I became an organized, focussed human being. Strictly speaking, organized and focussed were two words which had never applied to me, but I decided to accept the book in the spirit with which it was given and had read the tome from cover to cover well before the holiday had begun. Perhaps it needed to be read several times to produce the desired effect, as I found myself still caught up in the last minute dash to the shops during my lunch break on Christmas eve, followed by an extremely late night, wrapping the presents I had meant to do weeks ago.

But today was the start of a new year; I would begin to get my house in order, metaphorically as well as physically. An early spring clean wouldn't be amiss, getting rid of the clutter from the festivities of the last few days. Was it too early to take down the tree? Hmm, it was a scrawny specimen with more needles on the carpet than on the branches, yes it would have to go, out with the old and in with the new. Hey, that could be my mantra for the New Year, it had quite an efficient ring to it, 'out with the old and in with the new'. Yes, I rather like that and I'm sure Melissa-Jayne Frostbite would approve.

By seven am I had cleared away the debris in the kitchen and lounge. It amazes me how guests are so keen to stay to the bitter end of a good party, but suddenly feel they've out-stayed their welcome when you begin to clear up the mess. Still, I only made a token effort before the call of my cosy bed overtook my good intentions. Of course next year will be totally different, I'll have worked out the most efficient way to throw a party and achieve minimal disruption into the bargain, but for now perhaps I've earned a coffee and a bacon sarnie for breakfast.

Opening the fridge presented another dilemma. Left over cheesecake, those bite-sized chocolate éclairs and a tempting assortment of cheeses called out to me. Gosh, I didn't expect to face such a massive problem so soon into my new improved life. What would Melissa-Jayne

Flapjack do? Probably sacrifice the goodies to the dustbin and reach for the prunes. Maybe I could eat the left overs today and begin my new regime tomorrow, my mother always said it was a sin to waste good food while millions across the world were starving. The cheesecake was a little dry but two cups of coffee made it more than palatable. I resisted the cheeses, saving them for lunch to supplement the filo pastry tartlets and left over quiche. I could easily justify eating the left overs for two very good reasons, firstly the waste thingy and secondly because I didn't have any fresh, healthy options in the fridge. I would find a supermarket later in the day and stock up on caffeine free coffee, high fibre cereals, fresh fruit and veg. Yummy!

Inevitably the tiredness caught up with me and despite the gallon of coffee, I succumbed to the lure of my bed and by mid morning was fast asleep with Lucy curled up beside me, a furry, purring hot water bottle.

The telephone woke me at mid-day, or was it the door bell? Crumbs, it was both and as Lucy made no attempt to answer either, I struggled to the door snatching up the phone on the way. Strangely the perpetrator of both disturbances was my sister, Harriet, who claimed I wasn't answering the door bell so she just had to ring me from her mobile. It had not, of course, occurred to her that I might be sleeping, if she was up then the rest of the human race should be too.

"You must have stayed up late to clear the mess up." She observed.

"Actually no, I was up rather early and had just settled down for a little catch up."

She gave me one of those tight-lipped smiles which I know means she doesn't believe me, but hey, another of my resolutions had been not to let my big sister wind me up. I took a deep breath and returned her smile.

"Coffee?" I asked.

"Green tea if you have it." She replied, knowing full well that I wouldn't. Harry settled on Earl Grey and I joined her, resisting the urge to rummage in the cupboards to find a kit-kat to go with it.
"Well Alicia, how are you getting on with the life-coaching?"
"Oh give me a break; it's only the first day of January for heaven's sake." The sharpness of my own voice took me by surprise, bang goes another resolution.
"But haven't you made your lists? Melissa-Jayne Fosdyke always recommends lists, sticking to them is vitally important if you want to succeed."
I sighed, mentally counting up the number of resolutions I had already broken. There was the unhealthy food, letting my sister get to me, going back to bed instead of using my time constructively and I hadn't even composed a single list. Looking down at my tatty bathrobe confirmed another breech of the master plan, I looked a total mess. Shame washed over me followed swiftly by a defensive stubbornness and a desire to throw my fluffy pink slippers at my sister. Why should I try to change my life, I was happy wasn't I? Perhaps this life-coaching thing was good for Harry but it certainly wasn't for me. I loved my life, comfy old slippers and having nothing in the fridge except chocolate and red wine.
I looked at my sister, always striving for perfection, pushing herself to the limit yet feeling not one iota happier for all her efforts.
"I love you Sis, but this life coaching, list making stuff isn't for me. Perhaps Melissa-Jayne Claptrap works for some people, but I'm not one of them."
My sister smiled, a genuine thoughtful smile, and then surprised me by suddenly hugging me as if she hadn't seen me for eons. Pulling away there were tears in her eyes as she said,

"I'm sorry Alicia, I'm the one who needs to change, I love you just the way you are, even when you frustrate me. I think I'm probably a little jealous of your carefree, relaxed attitude to life, forgive me please?"
We hugged again, differences acknowledged but accepted, exactly how sisters should be. I shuffled off to the kitchen to rescue my ancient moccasins from the bin then turned to my sister,
"Chocolate éclair Sis?"

The End

www.gillianjackson.co.uk

Other books by Gillian Jackson.

'The Counsellor'
Janet's secret is out but is it too late to reclaim her life?

'Maggie's World'
If you can't remember your own husband how do you know who to trust?

'Pretence'
Are Rae's nightmares simply dreams or long forgotten memories?

'The First Stone'
Would winning the lottery be your dream come true, or your worst nightmare?